W9-BXX-546

sky blues

ALSO BY **VICKI HENDRICKS**

Miami Purity   *Iguana Love*   *Voluntary Madness*

sky blues

VICKI HENDRICKS

ST. MARTIN'S MINOTAUR NEW YORK

www.minotaurbooks.com

Designed by Lorelle Graffeo

ISBN 0-312-28346-6

First Edition: February 2002

10   9   8   7   6   5   4   3   2   1

To skydivers everywhere,

who understand that intensity of life

is worth the risk

acknowledgments

THANKS TO MY MANY SKYDIVE instructors, who got me through AFF alive those four years ago, enabling me to write this book and enjoy the most exciting time of my life. And to all my friends at Air Adventures in Clewiston and World Skydive Center in Lake Wales for being their crazy selves—and a special thanks for not being pissed at me to some of you whose names I couldn't fit in or thought I did but forgot. Thanks to Caleb for his expert checking—okay, I believe you that the raindrops theory is a myth, but I had to keep it. Thanks, Jerry and Jason C., for your advice on murder, and Lee and Lester, for all the smooth openings. Keep it up!

THANKS FOR THE QUICK LESSONS in veterinarian medicine from my college roommate, Denise Fuciu, D.V.M., as well as relentless inspiration over the years, and to Maude La Fortune, D.V.M., for the informative tour of Lion Country Safari.

OF COURSE, THANKS TO MY EDITOR at St. Martin's, Kelley Ragland, for squeezing one more scene out of me!

THE CHARACTERS, EXCEPT FOR Tom, Destiny, Roth, and Swan, are real, but the scenes are pure invention. The following is a list of other great people whom I couldn't include in the novel: Chik, Laurie, Madison, Dave, Jane, Jeff, Kai, Ruben, Jack, Juan, Bruce, Sherman, Michael, Glenn, Shakey, Lester, Brian, Keith, Bill, Stephanie, Andy, Sharon, Heidi, Adam, Martin, Mike, Patrick, Tiffany, Carl, Fred, Erica, George, Adriana, Tracy in South Africa, Kari Ann in Norway, and all my new friends at Skydive Chicagoland in Hinkley, Illinois. Blue skies always!

Why gamble with your money when you can gamble with your life?

—Anonymous, from a skydiver T-shirt

chapter

ONE

A DOG HOWLS HIS ASS OFF FROM the back kennel, and a raging burn of thirty-foot flame crackles in the cane field across the road. Black smoke rises in a column through the breezeless, humid sky. Yet there's still no relief from the relentless October sun that cuts a path across my office desk, where I sprawl, eyes stinging and stomach grinding with loneliness. I'm stuck here in the sticks of Central Florida with enough sun, smoke, and emptiness for anybody's interpretation of hell. I can expect a long season of this, frequent burns all around me, part of the sugarcane harvesting process. I check the clock and turn the other cheek down on the blotter, my dark, heavy hair a curtain against the brightness. Ten more minutes to rest before I head for Lion Country to start the day's fecal testing. My throat is raw from breathing in acrid fumes and exhaling despair.

It's a bastard of a dream come true—my new life in Pahokee, Florida, fucking sugar country on the lake. It's what I always thought I wanted, a private practice, to be the rural woman vet and make my way fearlessly, treating the animals—too much of *All Creatures Great and Small* as a child and a lack of good judgment as an adult. Living in the sticks—literally sticks of blackened cane—is god-awful, with no one even to listen to me complain. Suicide sounds delicious.

I hear the crunch of tires on the front drive. Damn it—I haven't locked up. I'm not in the mood to pull another goat fecal— payment next month—as per usual. I keep my head down and hope I've imagined it. Fat chance. The door to the waiting room creaks open and there's some clanging and banging, paint being chipped off my door frame. I straighten up, run my fingers across my lips to check for drool from when I dozed, and head out there.

I get a jolt as I step into the waiting room. This guy's a six-foot blond in a long-sleeved cotton shirt and nice soft-fitting jeans. He's got a chiseled face, a jaw so smooth, I want to stroke it. No way he's from Pahokee—I'd have seen him. He's got a lion cub in a metal cage that can barely hold it. Incredible. Heat rushes to my face. He rubs the animal behind the ears through the bars, soothing the victim of his selfishness. A shame. So drop-dead gorgeous and a goddamned animal abuser.

He looks up and his blue eyes almost knock me down.

"Sorry, ma'am, I don't have an appointment. Took a chance."

"Just in time," I say, hoping he'll confuse my flippant tone for enthusiasm. I open the door to the examination room and point the way, settle myself down. "You're lucky. I was just getting ready to leave."

He walks in, sets the cage on the table, and turns back to me. "I'm always lucky."

I twitch at this, and a smile blooms brilliantly across his face, white teeth welcoming. Obviously, he expects me to swoon. I'll manage not to. It is difficult, between his looks and that poor cub. Quick in, quick out. That's how to handle it. The tomcat slyness, cockiness—unneutered male on the prowl—it's too much, too sure, too dangerous for my vulnerable state.

He clangs open the cage door and slides the twenty-five-pound lion cub onto the examination table like it was a mound of dough.

I jerk my head up. "Careful," I say.

Asshole—I want to let fly, but his eyes stop me. Goddamn, their blue is blinding—high beams—an eye color I've only seen in deaf white cats.

I swipe across my forehead to cut the glare, get a grip on the cub's neck fur. Blue Eyes puts an arm across its chest. He's got instinctive know-how and the knowledge of how far that will get him—nothing's out of his reach. These are traits I've always admired and cultivated. My glance falls on ostrich-skin boots below the table, spread wide in front of my scuffed white tennies. Hmm. I put my finger into the side of the cub's mouth and check its gums.

"New in Pahokee, huh?" he says. "How you like it?"

I smile. "Fine," I tell him. I wonder if he keeps a knife in those fucking boots. Christ. Jack Daniel's belt buckle, too. I move my stare away from that area. He looks me in the eye and I catch the sapphire sparkle again. Shit. Sugarland cowboy with blond hair falling down his forehead and a lion cub he thinks he can handle. Hard not to take an interest.

"This little guy has near chewed up all my leather furniture. Next thing, he'll gnaw through my container and use my lines for dental floss."

I give him a look out of the corner of my eye. "Huh?"

"My rig. I'm a skydive instructor over in Clewiston—the drop zone on Twenty-seven."

I cross my arms and step back. Too much. The attraction of pure physical confidence oozes toward me. Here's somebody who jumps out of a perfectly good airplane every day—and no doubt enjoys it. I straighten myself. "You're a little out of your neighborhood, aren't you? There must be a vet in Clewiston."

"Not for a lion cub. You come recommended."

"Oh?"

"Yeah, a keeper at Lion Country—I didn't get his name." He winks. "Said you could take care of all my problems."

I frown, pondering the innuendo that's causing heat to build in my chest. I'm also wondering which keeper. "If you're about to ask for removal of his front teeth—and claws—so you can keep him indoors, you can forget it. If you have any sense, you'll let me take this animal over to Lion Country and put him on the preserve—introduce him before his health has deteriorated."

Those blues focus in on me. "Can't do." He shakes his head. "Miss Doc—I brought him here for his health. He's been having diarrhea for a couple days."

"Okay." I take a breath. "Did you bring a stool?"

"No. I didn't think of it—sorry. Believe me, ma'am, the first thing I realized was how he needed space. I'd love to free him out there in the park. The problem is, he doesn't belong to me."

"Oh?" I don't believe him for a second, but he could sell me gator oil with those eyes. I shift my weight and cock a hip under my lab coat. "Whom does he belong to?"

"Stranger. A guy I met at Les's—a place down the road—about three weeks ago. He paid me two thousand bucks to take care of this fellow. He said he'd be back in a couple months. I wondered at the time if I should've done it." He turns those dazzlers on me again.

I blink and recover.

"Tell you the truth," he says, "I thought I'd get a side of beef and feed this cat cheap—make some extra bucks easy—I didn't realize the damage."

"Uh-huh," I say. I hold the cub's head with both hands and look at his pupils. I take the penlight out of my breast pocket and check his ears. "Has he had his vaccinations?"

The sky cowboy is watching me closely. "No. That's another reason I'm here."

I delve through the fur on the back of the cub's neck, feeling the richness of it, as I check for dehydration by the looseness of skin. I rub behind his ears. "You know, lions eat the whole animal, skin and bones included. Unless you've been giving him that, he's not getting the proper nutrition."

"Yeah? Where do I get it?" The frown on his face looks real.

"We use a special blend at the park—Nebraska Meat. I don't know if they sell retail. I can recommend some supplements that'll help for a while."

"I'd appreciate it. I don't want to endanger his health—no, ma'am." He puts his hand on my shoulder. I look up.

The shade of his eyes has deepened. He seems sincere. "I'd like to show you how grateful I am for your help. You ever think about doing a tandem jump?"

"What?"

"A tandem skydive. That's what I do for a living—take you strapped to my chest. People generally get a real kick out of it."

The cub starts to squirm, and I hold him against my side and wrestle my arm under his front legs. The thought of jumping out of a plane is running through my body—pleasurable in a frightening way. "Never occurred to me."

He winks. "You're not a wuffo, are you, Miss—Doc . . . Dr. Donne?"

I hold the stethoscope against the cub's fluffy chest. Take my time.

"Desi is fine," I say. "What's a wuffo?"

"That's somebody who says, 'Wha' fo' you wanna jump outta perfectly good airplane?'" He laughs and puts a firm hand on my shoulder again. "Are you?"

I force a chuckle. "No, I never said that in my life." I push my hair behind my ear and look up into his gaze, into something powerful and magnetic, a whole new concept for Central Florida. I shift the cub under my arms.

"Desi," he says. "Cool. Short for Destiny—I saw your sign. Will you be my destiny?"

I try to smile as if I haven't heard anything like it ever before. "A tyrant's authority for crime and a fool's excuse for failure."

"Huh?" He laughs.

"Destiny." I shrug. "Whatever limits us, we call destiny."

He looks at me.

"My mother used to spout quotes around the house. My parents were hippies—still are."

"Sorry, I don't know any quotes. I'm just dull old Tommy—Tom Jenks."

I look at his face. Obviously, he thinks he's the most exciting man alive. Damn close, but he'll never know it by me. "Not your fault," I tell him. I motion to the cub. "I'll move around to the back end if you can hold him by the shoulders."

"Sure." He hunches over the cub to hold him. His arm lies across the animal's furry side, the hair on it matching the cub's golden color.

"He's taken a hunk out of every piece of furniture I've got, and I still have over a month to go—if the guy shows up when he said."

I shake my head.

He strokes the cub's ears. My eyes follow his fingers.

"Can't return him. What's the next-best thing?"

I slide the fecal loop up the cub's anus to try for a stool. I pull it out. "Good boy. Struck it rich." It doesn't look loose. I pat the cub's rump. "Hold him a minute."

I take the stool sample into the lab and make up the syringes with the FRCPC and feline leukemia vaccines. When I come back, Tom the tomcat is bent down, pinning the cub with his chest. "He's bored on this table," he says.

"Yeah." Fuck, yeah, I want to say, and he's going to get a lot worse. I motion Tomcat to the rear and get a hold of the cub's shoulders. He's such a beautiful animal. It makes me mad. I look back at Tom. "I am a wuffo. Wha' fo' you wanna take a wild animal and keep him cooped up inside? How would you like it—living in a cell?"

I'm close to saying he probably has an informed opinion on that kind of accommodation. He's staring, and I feel the sweat breaking out on my upper lip. I take a deep breath. "Build him a big cage outside. I mean huge. Cut some substantial limbs for him to climb and scratch. I know you don't mean him any harm, but he needs to be put back in his natural environment very soon, before he develops serious deficiencies and behavioral disorders. You tell that SOB you got him from that he has no business doing whatever he's doing with this cub."

He looks up from under long golden lashes. "I'll tell him as soon as I see him. Promise."

I'm sure he's bullshitting. It's his cub. I want to go further, but heat is building on my scalp and I know it's time to make my exit before I let this motherfucking cocksucker know my full opinion of him and his obvious testosterone poisoning—nothing better to do than fuck with nature.

"He's in good health so far," I say. "You can wait up front while I check the stool."

He gives me a half-lidded little-boy look—does it well, a blond, innocent Elvis, sex oozing my way. Maybe he's twenty-six or twenty-seven, a year or two younger than I am.

He puts out his hand and I squeeze it. "Thanks," he says. "I bet we'll be running into each other. You ought to come down and try a tandem jump. Ask for Tommy. I'll give you a deal."

I tell him, "You bet," and roll my eyes, but he's still holding my hand, and a wash of excitement nearly takes my breath. He lets go. "Thanks," I say. "Maybe sometime."

I help him scoot the cub back into the cage, and I duck around the corner into the lab. I pick up a slide, but my brain flashes a vivid picture of bright blond hair and a smooth tan face. Probably spends most of his time in the hot sun. Fried brains. I need to get a pith helmet or something that covers, ditch the visor. I prepare the slide and check it. Nothing. Healthy little guy. I walk out to the waiting room. The tomcat's sitting in a chair with his long legs stretched out in front of him, watching the toes of his boots.

"You can go. He's clean."

He looks at me and nods like he knew it. The blue eyes light up the room. "You have a nice day, Desi."

I watch as he picks up the cage and glides through the door. Time to remove my eyes from his ass and put my legs in gear. That's that. I go to the back, splash my face, and head out for the rest of the day's work. So, he jumps out of planes. Might be something just to watch.

IT'S A BUSY WEEK, AS ALWAYS—
the fecal business is as hot as the weather. I wander through it all
in a steamy haze, nearly living inside myself. Friday, I get a message
on my machine. "It's Tommy," he says. "The cub won't eat. Threw
up and has diarrhea."

I know it can't be worms this fast. Could be something more
serious. I phone him for directions to go out there when I finish my
afternoon at Lion Country. His place is the other side of Clewiston,
at least a forty-five-minute drive, but he says he's really worried
and will greatly appreciate it. I can't help wonder just a little if
there isn't something else on his mind. It's on mine. I feel a spark of
life in my body for the first time all week.

I make the turn onto an unpaved one-lane road, as he
described. I've already passed alongside a cane field and now I'm
headed into the jungle. The fringes of scrub palms flap against my
car top, even though I stay to the center of the gravel path for fear
of driving in loose sand. I catch sight of his driveway too late and
pass it. He's outside flagging me down by the time I back up. Gravel
tire tracks lead to a trailer that blends into the foliage. It's snarled
in draping ficus roots, Florida holly, and Spanish moss. I remember
the three-foot ficus I had in my apartment in Ohio. It cost me forty
bucks and lived only two months. They're like weeds here.

Tom motions me to follow him past the trailer a few hundred
yards. I pull up next to a cage that's a good twelve feet square, a
hell of a nice setup. The tawny cub is asleep in partial sun, with his

paws through the bars. His hair shines, similar to his owner's. I park and watch Tom stroll over.

"Friend of mine happened to have this cage. Nice, huh?"

I cock my head at him. "Yeah, real nice. I haven't seen anything like this outside of a zoo."

"Just lucky. I'm a lucky guy."

He opens the padlock and lets me inside the cage. It's shaded in part by trees and half of a chickee roof. He has a forked branch of eight-inch diameter wedged in there. In the corner is a stainless-steel trough of what looks like Nebraska Meat and a white five-gallon bucket filled with clean water. The cub is on his side against the trough. His chest rises with regular breathing.

"I just put out fresh food, but he wasn't interested."

I'm amazed. "Looks like you spent some time and money on this."

"Ingenuity. I felt bad after what you said—like a real asshole. I'm handy when I set my mind to a problem."

I can't stop thinking about his unexpected response to my advice as I walk over to the cub and get out my instruments. The cub sleeps soundly. I don't see any diarrhea on the ground—or vomit. He yawns and stretches as I put the stethoscope to his side and listen to his clear breathing. I check his eyes, ears, gums, and throat.

"Seems fine. Help me hold him so I can take his temperature."

"Rectal?"

I raise my eyes. "Unless you've got him trained to hold it under his tongue."

Tom laughs. "Pretty smart-ass, aren't you, huh? Miss—Doctor."

I wipe the sweat off my forehead. "Sorry. I've been out at Lion Country all day trying to train the elephants to do their TB tests—something new. They have to take fluid into their trunks and deposit it in sterile bags—it's not a natural action."

"Don't have anything against a smart-ass, Doc. The smart-ass gene runs strong in my family. We're proud to have intelligence in our lower regions."

I laugh. I feel a rush of blood to my face. I forgot what flirting is like.

I show him how to hold the shoulders of the cub while I get my thermometer and lift the tail to get to the anus. "Got him?"

"Yep. Plug him."

I watch Tommy's long, slim fingers holding the cub in a firm, gentle grip. I keep the thermometer steady and look around at the cage again. It is a knowledgeable setup, amazing. I wonder if the cowboy is always so capable.

I check the thermometer and shake it down. "I can't see anything wrong here."

We let the cub go and he walks over to the food dish and begins to chow down. I look up at Tommy's face. So soft and smooth.

"Shit. Just like a kid, always makes you a liar. He wouldn't touch a thing for two days."

"Happens. I don't have an ego problem. I'm happy if the patient gets well without me."

"Hate to bring you out here for nothing."

I wipe the sweat off my neck. "Don't worry—I'm still gonna charge you for a house call."

He laughs. "You are a smart-ass. Sure—I'd insist on paying. I was just going to suggest a cold drink before you hit the trail. I open a great can of Bud."

I look at him in his clean T-shirt and cutoffs, those shining blond legs. He scratches behind his ear.

"You'll have to listen to my lecture on the dangers of keeping exotic pets."

"I can handle it."

He motions for me to follow him. We walk back along the path toward the trailer, but he turns off before we get there and leads me to a picnic table under a low-hanging ficus. The hairlike roots have been cropped above the table, leaving the outer fringe to hang down almost like a curtain. Tommy holds aside some strands for me to pass through and brushes dead leaves off the bench. Despite the humidity, it's comfortable in the shade.

"I like to sit outside starting in October—the seething heat is over and you can breathe. The trailer is pretty cramped."

"You must know how that cub feels."

He shakes his head like his brains are rattling. "There's not a word I can say that won't bring up something about that cub."

"Probably not. I warned you." I try to soften it with a smile.

"Hang on. No—second thought—just start without me. I'll catch up when I get back with the beers. How many? I'm having two real fast."

I hold up one finger—the middle one. I can't hold back a laugh.

"Cute. Does that mean one? I could take it another way." He gives me a look—as slow as he can—down my whole five-foot-two frame, from baggy T-shirt to stained jeans and sneakers. His eyes shift back to my tits. Yeah, I want to say, I have to buy my bras from the tent and awning shop. So what? I've had these monsters since birth—the rest of me just never caught up. I don't say anything. I stare back. He smiles and turns down the path.

We drink our beers and I give him my best lecture, but my mind isn't on it. I'm feeling too good, just watching his hands on the beer can, the endearing golden hairs on his fingers. He slides his index finger up and down in the condensation. My thoughts drift away and I stop talking.

He stands and walks slowly over to my side of the table. He motions me to get up quietly, taking my shoulders to point me toward a holly. He whispers that a roseate spoonbill has landed on a branch.

I know them from the park, but I can't see this bird he's pointing out. Tom pulls me to his chest and I feel his fingers on the back of my neck, massaging. I slump against him and let the sensation run through me as he makes his way down my spine and manipulates my lumbar. "Spoonbill must have flown," I mumble.

"You need some relaxing—a little TLC, like you've been giving all those animals." His hands stop and I look up, wanting more. He puts his mouth on mine and I melt under it. He lifts the heavy damp hair off my back and holds it while the cool breeze touches my neck and his tongue penetrates warm and hard between my lips. His fingers cup my head and slip into my ears. I'm floating in a sexual surge.

He stops. I look up, my mouth still open. His eyes are misty, lids half-mast with suggestion. His hands slide down my sides and come up under my T-shirt. "Umm, these are real," he says.

It makes me laugh—they've been in my way all my life. I sure didn't have money to spend on implants all those years when I couldn't afford dinner half the time—more likely, I'd have gone for a reduction. He and I are from a different universe. I swallow and breathe and gather myself. I pull back and take in his face. It's the soft, sweet facade of a studied womanizer. I know it. I'm no spring bunny just waiting to get jumped from behind. He thinks everything's so easy for him. I flip my hair back. "I've got a long drive home," I say.

He runs his fingers through the blond mane and straightens his jeans on his hips. I look toward the path.

"Think I might get you out one day for some fun? I work steady weekends, but I can make time during the week."

"I don't know," I tell him, my voice husky. Being without any masculine attention for months, I'm highly susceptible. A sensible relationship would be something to think about, not this. I don't know how to deal with his kind. I clear my throat and gather my hair, catch the sweaty strands. "I'm really busy at the office and with the park, but keep me posted on the cub."

chapter

THREE

October and still damn hot. I'm driving home from Lion Country, nearly dozing after a twelve-hour day of office calls, rhino immobilization and TB testing, and tons of paperwork catch-up. A tan Bronco pulls close behind me. I glance in the rearview mirror, to see the square jaw and smiling face of Tom the tomcat. I twitch. A tingle runs down my back. I'd almost forgotten about him—almost. The feel of his mouth has crossed my mind more than once when I was curled up in bed, drifting into dreamland.

His eyes hide under dark glasses, and he has an Aussie-type hat pushed back on his head so the blond hair spills down his forehead. He motions me to pull over. I wave and smile, looking at him in the mirror. He keeps motioning. I slow and pull over. He comes up alongside, his passenger window open.

I roll mine down.

"Hey, Dr. Destiny, we gotta stop meeting like this."

So cornball and unoriginal, it doesn't deserve acknowledgment. But I feel the surge of a blush coming up my neck. I don't know if it's his looks—or that up-front nerve. He needs testing and competition, although the only way to win is to leave him alone.

I realize I've been staring half a second too long.

"Long day," I yell. "Brain-dead. You're far from home, aren't you?"

He nods. "Business."

"How's that cub doing? The guy come back for him?"

"No, no. He's not due in yet. I got a name for the little bugger, though—Jeepers."

"Jeepers?"

"You know, 'Jeepers Creepers'? My little nephew saw him. He said, 'Jeepers, you sure are a big kitty!' It was between that and Bubba."

"Good choice," I yell. I try to picture him in a family setting. "You have a little nephew, huh?"

"Huh? Yeah. Hang on a sec."

I know I've asked for it now. Tomcat pulls his Bronco off the road in front of me and comes strolling back. He has a casual, graceful flow to him.

"Yeah, my brother's kid—six years old, spoiled rotten. Crazy about animals—wants to be a vet when he grows up."

I turn off my engine. "You better be careful. He might try to visit 'the kitty' when you're not around. That would be extremely dangerous."

"Don't worry. I don't leave him there alone. Hey, Doc, I'm smarter than that."

"How should I know?"

"Shit."

"Sorry—I've heard too many stories—people's well-intentioned ignorance."

He puts his arms on my window ledge and his face inside the cab. I feel his breath. He smells like he's just had a shower.

"Good thing I found you for my lecture of the week."

"Sorry." I shake my head. I'm thinking he missed last week's.

"You do jump to conclusions—very poor judge of men."

I laugh. "Look—if you want, we could arrange for me to take your nephew— what's the little guy's name?"

"Bradley, but we call him Bubba."

"Oh. Well, I could take him to the park one day and show him around, give him a special tour and a little education about the animals."

"He'd love it. I might like it, too."

I see his devilish wink but refuse to go further with that thought.

"Call me at the office and we'll set it up for Saturday," I say. A look slips across his face. I know he works on Saturdays, and I'm ruining his maneuver. He must have a million women anyway. "Tell Bradley's mother I'll pick him up."

"Gottcha."

I turn the key and motion him aside, wipe my forehead. "I'm dead."

He blows a kiss and steps back. He walks over to his truck, and I pull around him and wave. His wide smile shows a lot of beautiful teeth. I can feel his eyes following me down the road. He doesn't move as long as I can see.

chapter

FOUR

THAT NIGHT, IT'S TOUGH GETTING to sleep, even bushed as I am. I have mixed feelings about whether I should have invited Bradley to the park. The tomcat's just trying to get a personal connection. He is certainly a looker, and clever, and a nicely enough mannered guy, but I know I'm being worked, probably the only woman in the county who hasn't crawled under him yet. I don't like feeling manipulated and out of control.

I turn the pillow to get the cool side, try to settle my head. "Takes one to know one" comes to mind. I'm not innocent of maneuvers. It haunts me that I might never have gotten into vet school without a short fling with the head of the committee—frisky-fifties John Manners, D.V.M. I could be wrong, but I'll never know. My grades and references were perfect, but so were a lot of people's. I lived for that acceptance and I wasn't sure women were getting a truly fair shake. There was still a feeling of the "weaker sex." A guy in ag class once told me that at five feet tall, a hundred pounds wet, I wouldn't be capable of working on large animals. He said he'd take my spot. I told him, "Fuck you—if a squirrel crawled up your leg, it would starve." But he made me realize that if I didn't have control over how my femininity worked against me, I should make sure it worked equally for me. The chance soon sprang into my lap. It was in the last year before I was ready to apply to vet school. I met Manners, a close friend of Dr. Greer's, the vet where I worked as an assistant. I never mentioned my future plans to him. Manners was married and didn't ask anything about my life.

It was fine with me. He was my break between work and study. I get warm feelings thinking about it. I enjoyed his cock. I rode it or sucked it, at the same time envisioning myself in my lab coat at a table in my own office, treating a German shepherd with hip dysplasia, freeing it from pain and restoring its spirit. Manners didn't balk when I hit him with the deal. I promised no trouble with his wife if I got in. The smoothness of his agreement almost made me think he'd gone that route before. Could have been he knew about me all along from Dr. Greer, and I was the one being used—shit, we were both using each other. I'd gotten attached to him anyway, missed him when it was over. From there on, it was pure determination and discipline that kept my scholarship. I did without entertainment and clothes and got by on a spoonful of peanut butter for dinner plenty of times. I paid my price, but I still feel the twinge of guilt.

Now, when security and a life of respect is finally in reach, I don't need to start juggling a hot poker. I wonder if Tommy thinks I have money, a financial plan to support his hobbies.

I get a call the next day. Tom explains that Bradley's family had already planned a weekend trip to visit grandparents, and the next Saturday, the boy is supposed to get braces. He says Bradley overheard the conversation with his mother and spent the afternoon teary-eyed, with his bottom lip stuck out. Tom wonders if we could set up a quick trip on a weekday afternoon. That way, *he* can also join us!

He knows I'm whipped. I can't disappoint the little guy, so I ignore my gut feeling and tell Tom that Wednesday at three will be fine, although Bradley won't get to do rides or see many of the other attractions. Tom says he'll bring Bradley to the office to save time.

I wonder if I can keep Tom from figuring out that I have living quarters in the rear. I feel my bed lurking. I know he'll drop Bradley off on the way back, and we'll arrive here alone.

Wednesday is my monthly free neutering and spaying day. I finish suturing the last male at 2:45, just enough time to run to the back, check my elbows for dried blood, splash my face, and put on a little blush. I change into a pair of khaki shorts and an outback-type shirt. I notice the sheets are rumpled. No—what am I thinking? I don't make the bed.

Despite my apprehensions, I can't help being excited about an afternoon with a hunk. It's been months since I've been with a man for fun.

I'm giving my hair a few whacks with a brush when I hear the bell. They're three minutes early.

We ride over in Tom's Bronco, with Bradley in the backseat, chattering nonstop. He's a cute little blond and keeps the questions coming. Twice the tomcat winks and manages to touch my shoulder with his fingers. The seat is long enough that he can't quite reach my neck. I raise my brows at him the second time. Bradley catches on and pokes me and winks. I wink back at him. Fast learner. Probably a family trait.

When we reach the gate, Tom insists on paying admission rather than letting me take them in free. He says he wants to contribute to a business that shows moral responsibility for the treatment of animals.

My eyebrows lift.

He doesn't blink. "I'm not an insensitive slug, hon," he says.

I jerk at the "hon" and he winks. "Dr. Hon."

I give up.

It's good day for me to do rounds, so we park his Bronco and cut through the gate to stop at my office in the Care Center to get my radio. I ask them to wait a few minutes while I set up some medication for the keepers to administer later that evening. Bradley is looking around and sees the riflelike dart guns.

"Uncle Tom has one of them."

I laugh. "Uncle Tom? I wouldn't think so," I tell him.

"Uh-huh."

I look at Tom. He shakes his head. "Bradley, no arguing."

"These are dart guns, not hunting rifles." I lift one down to show them, and then the metal ones I have, and the Telinject darts. Tom is interested in how they work, and I point out the side opening in the needle and the ring that seals it. "On impact, the ring slides back and allows the liquid to enter the animal subcutaneously."

"Cool. It's hard for me to picture a little lady like you out shooting an elephant or a rhino," Tom says. "It's kinda sexy, though."

I give Tom a frown. "I don't shoot anything." I look at Bradley. "You understand that, right? The dart has medicine to make the animal better."

He nods. "Uh-huh. I wish I could shoot one."

Bradley walks over and looks into the cage on my desk. "Whose mouse is this?" he asks.

"Mine. It's a domestic white rat."

Tom looks over. "Don't stick your fingers in there."

"She's tame. I've had her since vet school. See her leg. She was injured."

Bradley and Tom peer into the cage. "She's got no foot," Bradley says.

"She used to be the fastest maze runner at the university. Then some students put her in with another rat, and it chewed her foot off. They'll chew on anything," I tell Tom. The look on his face suggests that I'm weird. I grin. "We had to change her name from Nimblefoot to Nibblefoot."

I laugh and Tom meets my eyes. He's still teasing me with a strained look, but there's something like admiration behind it.

"Nibblefoot." Bradley giggles.

I get the tray of syringes I've prepared, and Tom watches while I gather a few more things. "Can anybody get those dart guns?" he asks. "Seems dangerous."

"Certainly not. You have to be licensed—people try to steal this stuff."

"What for?"

"Actually, not the succinylcholine—M-99. That's for tranquilizing rhinos. Just the residue on the end of a needle will put you into respiratory arrest in a minute—you have to wear gloves and shields, definitely not a high. But we also use Ketamine—known as Special K on the street. Vets get robbed all the time."

"Drug dealers steal those darts?"

"No, no. We get it in powder form, prepare it for whatever size syringe or dart we need. The park was broken into once before I started working here."

"Hmm. You have access to all the drugs you want, huh?" He winks.

I glance at Bradley, who's poking at Nibble. "The FDA keeps records. Not my style anyway."

I motion the boy toward the door. He puckers up and gives Nibblefoot a kiss on top of the cage. We walk out to my little black-and-white-striped truck to do a round through the five sections of animals.

Bradley runs ahead. "Cool, a zebra truck," he yells. He strokes the stripes as we walk up. "You oughta get Aunt Swan to buy you one of these," he says to Tom.

I walk toward the driver's side, wondering who Aunt Swan is—Tom's sister? Tom reaches over to Bradley and gives him a noogie. Bradley screeches. I open the door and he scoots in. Tom looks at me across the top of the cab. "Swan is on the money side of the family. Bradley thinks she buys everything for everybody."

"No I don't," Bradley calls. "Mommy said—"

"Hey, Bubba," Tom hollers. He gets into the truck and puts a finger on each corner of Bradley's mouth, pinching it to make fish lips. "Okay, Bubba. That's enough back talk. Let's enjoy the trip. It's not everyday we can get a private tour with a beautiful lady."

I back out and turn to head into section one. I'm thinking, *Swan*—with a name like that, she must have hippie parents like mine, only rich.

Lake Nakaru shimmers in the heat and wispy clouds hover in the blue sky. The emus and rheas are picking at the turf, their fuzzy feathers not even moving in the stillness. A group of marabou storks stands rigid near the road, looking like the carrion-eaters they are.

"It's just like their natural habitat," I tell Bradley. "We take good care of them and they live longer than in the wild." I point out the monkey islands in Lake Nakaru. A blond white-handed gibbon is hanging by one hand, watching us.

"Uh-oh," Tom tells Bradley. "He looks just like you. Better be good or we might trade you in."

I pat Bradley's leg and frown at Tom. "Don't tell him that."

"He knows I'm just kidding. Don't you, sport?"

Bradley nods. "Where're the lions? I wanna see some big ones."

I do a quick run through the hoof stock in section two. I know the keepers generally have the updates on all the animals and they'll let me know if I need to check on any new problems. I point out some Dall's sheep to Bradley, the males and females identified by tags in their ears. The lambs are frisky, as usual.

"In the wild, some of these lambs would die," I tell Bradley, "because the mother will only care for one, and they're usually born in twos or threes. Here we take them to the nursery and raise them."

"Can I have one?" he asks. "I could keep it at Uncle Tom's."

"Nope. Sorry." Tom turns to me. "The little beggar is really amped today."

In the preserve, I point out Norman, one of the big male lions I know by name. He's stretched out under a tree close to the road. I tell them how we had to immobilize all these animals to bring them to the new section one by one in a trailer behind the truck. The other lions would spot the truck coming through the gate and follow. "It was creepy, Tom. We have nearly twenty lions, and after a few transports, I was like the Pied Piper. These guys always know what's going on."

"Good act. Looks like they're flat out sawing logs."

"Yeah. Normally, they sleep twenty hours a day and eat the rest of the time—that's their job. Once in awhile, they fight over spots, though. Bite lacerations are the most common injuries."

We drive through the gate to the next section. We pass plenty of napping ostriches with their heads on their backs and a water buffalo in the road, a group of beautiful gemsbok with their painted faces in striking black designs, the giraffes, the zebras. I see a wound on one giraffe's leg—Valentine's—it's a chunk of flesh about the size of my palm, somehow sliced off. The gap's filled with dirt. I radio to the keeper to keep Valentine in her night stall the next morning so I can squirt out the cut with the hose and dart her with some antibiotic.

I tell Bradley there's one more thing to make this day special. The two lion cubs are due for their third vaccination, and he can watch. "Their names are Bora and Kimya, a male and female, a little older than Jeepers—three months, thirty-four and thirty-three pounds," I tell Tom. "Getting more difficult to handle."

I drive us back to get the vaccines from the refrigerator at the hospital and I call on the radio for two keepers to help with the holding. The cubs are too strong already for me to do it alone. I can't let Tom and Bradley into the cage, for fear of liability against the park.

When we get to the nursery cage in the amusement section, I let them stand in the back section. The keepers and I throw a towel over the cubs' furry blond heads, one by one, and pump the syringe quickly into their shoulders. The male lets out a loud ghostly growl and gets a bite on my ass. It doesn't penetrate my heavy shorts—just a playful nip. I hear Tom laughing a little nervously.

I go back out, leaving the women keepers playing with the cubs, handing out treats to make them forget the sting.

"Frisky male," I tell Tom, and nod toward the cage.

"Thanks."

"No—the cub—"

He laughs and I punch him on the shoulder, nice firm shoulder. Our eyes meet. There's a pause. I'm aware of my breathing.

He winks. "How do you tell them apart—besides looking at their gear?"

"By size. If I didn't see them together, I might not be able to. As they get older, they develop more markings."

We continue to walk past the cages of animals. "I can see you need all three people to give those shots."

"Yep. Soon, you'll need three people to handle Jeepers."

"I better check that bite you got—see if you need a little first aid."

I feel my face redden at the appeal of his suggestion, but I try not to show my interest. I look at Bradley to see if he's taking this in. He's looking ahead at Redman, the ninety-year-old tortoise.

I turn to Tom. His eyebrows go up and down, like he thinks I'm going to give him a peek at my ass. My face gets hotter. I suppress all feeling. "I'm fine, thanks."

We get back to the Care Center and I give them a quick tour of the few animals that are caged for problems.

"We let them stay in their habitat as much as possible. They recover much more quickly that way. They only come here if the others would cause them further injury or they need close observation."

We enter the covered cement shelter and pass some empty

chain-link stalls. "We put the parrot in here at night so the rac-coons don't get him."

We walk to the end of the row and I open a padded chain-link door to show them an eland. The soft beige face of the antelope tilts toward us. I point out the gym pads covering the walls completely. "They tend to bounce around. This way, he can't get hurt."

"Cool. Huh, Bubba?" Tom says to Bradley.

There's nothing more to see, so I lead them back out into the sunshine. "The keepers all know their own animals, many by name. They tell me if I need to check on something. Animals can hide their illnesses until they're far gone. In the wild, to show weakness is to invite attack."

"Makes sense for everybody," Tom says.

"I don't know." I laugh. "For men maybe."

"Women, too, huh? I know you believe that."

I shrug. "I have some fecals to catch up on. Want to take Bradley through the rest of the amusements while I finish up? There're a lot of reptiles and birds, a petting zoo, too."

They go out. I wipe my face with a paper towel and put my first slide on the microscope. I scan for ascarids, but I'm thinking about Tom. I wonder if he assumes I'm scared of him. Odd comment. Or maybe I seem to be showing off, talking too much about what I do. I open the next plastic bag and put some rhino droppings on the slide. This one's got them. The rhinos have been heavy on the nematodes lately. I need to do a sweep. Hit them all with a dose.

I really don't care what Tom thinks. This is the job I've worked toward all my life. I go to the cabinet and check for darts and med-ication, see if I need to order anything. Swan. Pretty name—although the bird itself has a nasty temperament. A money side to the family—might explain where that nice cage came from.

WE DROP BRADLEY IN HIS DRIVE-
way and wait until the little squirt opens the door. He turns and
blows me a kiss.

Tom laughs. "He's trying to steal you right out from under me."

I don't know how to reply to that. If I say I'm not under him, it
could sound like I'm weaseling to get there. It's hard to deny I want
it—I'm near saying to hell with caution, but probably he talks this
way to all the women.

"We did good," Tom says. "Got him home just in time for dinner. He had a great time."

I notice Tom likes to play up his country-boy style. That
smooth, slight drawl of his can soften anything, create an invitation.

My eyes have drifted over his body all day. His skin is tan, with
those shining hairs on his arms and fingers, and his face has a
small-pored smoothness and prominent bone structure that will
keep him beautiful all his life. From the looks of him, he couldn't
have picked better genes if he tried. I'm surprised he isn't married.
Maybe living in that trailer put off the women. You'd think they'd
be crawling all over him.

"Want to stop for a drink? Your turn to buy me a beer, hon."

"Oh yeah?"

"How 'bout I buy you dinner? Good catfish joint down the
road. You gotta eat."

I realize my stomach is hollow, and it pushes me over the line.

We pull up in front of Tom's BBQ and I smell the hickory smoke curling out of the chimney. It beckons me, even though I don't eat ribs, hadn't even considered eating a large animal for years. I point to the sign. "This your place? I didn't know you could cook."

"I wish. They do a hell of a business."

He holds the door. As I pass him, I get the warm feeling that comes from having somebody big and strong and male within a few inches. No matter how corny or superficial the action, just the physical presence of him walking behind me gives me pleasure I haven't much allowed myself. It's a short road from there to trouble. I feel it.

They have the catfish he promised, and it's crisp and tender. I watch him tear into a rack of ribs. He cleans those bones with neat expertise, and he doesn't miss a fleck of sauce as he wipes up with his napkin. He divides up the rest of the pitcher of beer, and I'm as gone as a dog on Ace.

I'm feeling friendly enough to share my food. I point to the crunchy fries still on my plate. "Help yourself."

"I like that invitation."

Warmth moves up my neck. It feels good. I laugh. "I meant the fries."

He grabs a fry and sticks it up his left nostril. He looks across the table at me, waiting for a reaction, then pulls it out and eats it. "Saw that in a movie."

It's a crazy, unexpected side of him. I hold in a laugh and wonder why I'm not repulsed. "I'll ask for some ketchup, if you'd like."

He gives a casual shake of his head. "No thanks. It's all natural."

In the car on the way to my place, I can barely keep from bubbling into some sort of adolescent giggle. He's such a charmer. A fry in the nose hole—I wonder if he intended it to be phallic.

He pulls up in front of the office and I reach for the door handle. I'm fumbling when his arm comes across and turns my head.

His mouth locks onto mine and I'm there. It's a drug. His fingers press hard into my neck and scalp, holding me in rapture. My skin radiates heat, and the gravity of one body for another melds me to his chest. I'm overwhelmed with the intensity of touch and my eyes and ears are muffled. He finally pulls back to get out of the car. The eighty-degree air that replaces him is chilly. I feel for my purse and smooth back my hair. I can hardy wait the seconds till he opens my door and drags me out faster than I can step, my feet barely grazing the ground.

I hear the dogs in the kennel barking, and my own two—Angel and Clue, a mixed-breed shepherd and rottweiler—in the kitchen of the apartment. I lead the way as swiftly as I can, bumping against his hip, trying not to fall off the edge of the sidewalk into the soft sand and fecal land mines I haven't had time to clean up. The sun is just setting and I smell the jungly moisture of evening.

I turn the knob on the side door and shove. "Back, back," I say. I push the two furry heads inside and Tom wedges in behind me.

"These are my kids," I tell him.

The dogs stop barking and start to whine for my attention, so I reach a hand down and touch each head. Tom swoops, and I'm caught up. I lash my arms around his neck and plaster my mouth on his. He starts moving down the wrong hall, toward the laundry room, till I get a breath and point him back the right way. I gasp between kisses, "The bed's not made. . . . The sheets need changing." He laughs and buries his mouth in my neck. If I don't survive the intensity of this, I don't care.

I land on the rumpled covers, but his mouth stays on my neck. I feel his firm body pile on top of me, his split thighs pinning my hips, fingers holding my head at the angle where his mouth can reach the most skin, sending electricity through my brain. My face is in his soft blond waves, and the clean scent of his shampoo drags me further into him. My hips rise against his abdomen and I can feel his full cock pressing my pubic bone.

He lifts his head and starts unbuttoning down my chest. I go under his arms to his leather belt with the Jack Daniel's buckle and pull out the flap, bend it back, see the glint of the tiny metal prong, and finally unhook it and undo the button and zipper. No underwear. After months of looking at small pointed animal penises, it's like an unveiling, completely new, beautiful in its power and tenderness. I slide my fingers over the taut pink satin skin and smooth circumcised head. Saliva comes into my mouth.

He peels back my shirt and strips down the bra, and I yank at his pants with one hand. I continue to stroke the smooth skin while his face goes over my nipples, and my shorts move down to my knees and off. I open my thighs and watch him pull his pants off smooth tan hips. He finds a condom in his pocket—no surprise that he's prepared—and I wait, grateful and impatient, while he smooths it on. Finally, he hunches down and angles his hips. I take a deep, hot breath as I feel him slip inside and plunge through the slippery wetness into the needy well of my vagina—nearly forgotten but instantly revived. The push and drag send me moaning into a better world. I'm near to unconscious when I hear his deep groan and feel him center on me. I melt into the bed.

It's dark when I wake up. I make out Tom moving around the bed, picking up his clothes.

"You're welcome to stay. I don't get started till eight tomorrow."

He bends down and kisses me, strokes my hair. "No. You'll get a better night's sleep without me. I know how you hardworking, independent women don't like to be crowded."

"Oh yeah? You're right."

He pulls the covers from under me and brings the sheet up over my chest, kisses my forehead. "I think I can find my way out."

"Thanks. Take care." I yawn. "Watch out for dog shit."

"One of the hazards of making love to a vet."

" 'Hmm. . . . Especially when you leave in the dark."

"Let's try an afternoon soon."

"I'm pretty busy. Tempt me."

He gives me one more kiss and goes out. I hear him womp into Clue in the hall, but nobody's hurt. His steps go through the kitchen and the door clicks shut.

I roll onto my side and curl up. I don't know about this. I really don't know. Right now, I don't care.

I WAKE UP FEELING CLEAR-MINDED on the following Wednesday, accepting the fact that I haven't heard from Tom in a week. I got exactly what I needed—a good fuck, no complications. Yet I feel edgy. The problem is, my passion has revived, and there's nobody else in range even of my imagination. But it's clear to see I'm better off the way it's turned out, no feeling of manipulation or whatever it was I suspected. Yet all morning, I replay moments of him in my head.

Later, I'm lancing a sebaceous cyst on a large black Lab—named Bubba, of course. The phone rings. Corey, my assistant, is on an errand, so I let the voice mail pick up. I have a feeling it's Tom—the workings of fate, a cosmic joke of timing, just when I'm feeling fine about not seeing him. As I finish up on the dog and take his owner's Visa, I convince myself it would be a mistake to go out with Tom again—if I do get the chance. I help the woman get Bubba out the door and into the car. I head for the phone.

It's Tom all right. He says he wants to invite me to do a skydive, a tandem with him—his treat. He'd planned to call sooner, but he wanted to be sure he could work me into his schedule on Saturday afternoon. My feeling of pleasure is so intense that I dial him and accept, before rational thought can stop me.

By Saturday at 3:30, I've neutered and spayed and sutured up six cats, and gotten myself to the little airport on time. I'm feeling trim and energetic as I cut across the grass to the entrance of Air Adventures. I've got on my best-fitting shorts, a snug cotton top, and new white socks and sneakers. I feel good looking down at the fresh white leather, instead of blood and dung stains. I'm thinking, It does me good to pay a little attention to my appearance.

I step inside and catch sight of Tom. He's so gorgeous, he nearly glows across the room. I realize how much I've been affected by the sex. I concentrate on breathing normally. He shoots me a smile and I get a rush of sweet feelings that aren't called for.

He's in a zippered jumpsuit of white and aqua, a sleek super-hero, with the hair, eyes, and square jaw. He doesn't look like a cowboy at all without the belt and boots. "Hey, hon, come on over." He motions me from behind the counter and I walk quickly, conscious of every step.

"Glad you made it." He leans and gives me a peck on the cheek. It's friendly, no innuendo in front of the woman and other guys behind the desk. "Perfect timing," he says. "I'm almost done for the day. Afterward, we can have a drink to celebrate."

I save my no for later. He's all business. He hands me several printed sheets of paper. "Fill these out while I make sure we're set for video with Neil." He leans and whispers in my ear. "How bout a nude jump?"

I open my mouth, but he's already moved out of range.

I take the forms to a table and sit down, consciously slowing my breathing, and begin reading the release. I have to sign and initial at least a dozen places to ensure that I understand all the risks and that neither I nor my family will hold anybody liable if I die.

When I finish, I go back to Tom at the desk. "Okay. My life is in your hands."

"Good choice," he says. He winks. It scares me. I've just consented to every detail of impending doom. I'm about to throw myself out of a plane, strapped to this man I barely know. What if the straps break? What if neither chute opens? Tom takes me over to a setup of chairs and a couch in front of a big-screen TV. I sit next to a couple who will be going up on the same trip. I feel jittery—open sky, hard ground—but it's a good feeling in part, to be alive and yet have the startling awareness of death. I've never taken such a risk knowingly. Large animals are nothing by comparison, just hooves and horns to worry about. I focus on what will come after, if I live—a skydive and a jump with Tom, a Saturday to remember. It's the only life in Central Florida. I've already chosen.

A big blond guy comes out and stands in front of the TV. He's like a bear. "I'm Neil," he says. He's holding a tape. "I'll be doing your video. In a minute, I'll show you the training film, so you'll have a safe, exciting skydive."

He explains the high qualifications of all the tandem instructors—thousands of jumps—and shows me a piece of the nylon strapping. "All you have to do is count to three and open out like a bird. Your instructor will do all the rest." I'm wondering if I'll be able to remember even such brief instructions.

He turns on the video. "We have a perfect record—zero fatalities." I flinch at the word. He stands aside and the sound comes up. A guy with a long beard, sitting at a desk, begins to talk about liability. No sugar coating, no squeamishness about the words *death* and *dismemberment*. The camera swings to people walking and follows them into the airplane—a small yellow bird with doors open straight through the center. Jumpers boost themselves inside. The narrator has changed and the mood is light. The camera scans the inside of the plane and out the window. The plane climbs fast. The camera moves in on Tom's face looking over the head of a woman who smiles weakly. Tom smiles and clowns with fingers in his ears, beaming, an attitude of "You can't catch me." Tempting fate isn't enough—he has to poke fun at it.

The music changes to something soothing. Tom becomes serious and considerate as he checks the straps and motions gently to his guest. The movement is smooth and sexual as they scoot, locked together, toward the door of bright blue space, Tom moving her easily and gracefully.

"Ready?" he asks. His lips read clearly. "Okay," she says. He smiles and they're out. I can't tell if he pushed or if she went willingly. She flattens into a layout with her arms straight, legs between his. A small, round parachute goes up from his back. "That's the drogue," Neil says. She faces the camera. Her cheeks are indented by the wind, her nose turned up, mouth frozen in a smile. Tom's face, inches above her head, is a show of white teeth and dancing brows. He takes her arms and waves them wildly. She appears to be having fun.

The camera stays with them as she says something. Their cheeks and jumpsuits flap. They turn a little one way and then the other, seemingly suspended by the cord of the tiny parachute, not falling at 120 mph as I've been told. Tom's hand goes down slowly and purposely and pulls the ripcord on her hip. They seem to jerk upward, almost out of sight.

Neil turns down the volume and points to the screen. "Don't worry. There's no hard jolt, just a slowdown of the tandem while the cameraman keeps falling."

In the next scene, Tom and the woman come back into view at a distance, drifting downward slowly to the ground, where the cameraman is already waiting.

"You can pull the ripcord or let the jumpmaster do it." He smiles and dimples show. "If you lose it, it's twenty dollars." I make a mental note to pull my own cord. I want the whole experience if I'm going this far.

Tom and his tandem come in closer, almost on the ground, crossing the tarmac. Tom takes one step from the air and lands lightly in the middle of a circle. The camera zooms in on their grins. The rainbow nylon of the chute collapses behind them in a cascade of fluffy color. Such a beautiful sport, so visually benign from the ground.

"Nothing to it," Neil says.

He starts filming as Tom and I walk into the open hangar. We pass a guy wearing a T-shirt that says WHY GAMBLE WITH YOUR MONEY WHEN YOU CAN GAMBLE WITH YOUR LIFE? Neil grins and films the shirt. I try to chuckle. We go to a rack of jumpsuits and Tom helps me into one, a perfect guess at my size. He winks. I watch as he gears up, and we both smile for the camera.

"Are we having fun yet?" Neil asks. He turns toward Tom.

"You bet," says Tom. His voice gains some volume and drama. "I'm taking Dr. Destiny up for her first tandem, but I bet it won't be her last jump."

I groan. "Des will do."

He turns a wide grin on me and I have to smile back. Neil turns the lens directly at my face. "How are you feeling, Doc?"

"A little nervous—"

"It wouldn't be any fun if you weren't," Tom says. He puts his hand on my shoulder and moves close for the camera. "We're gonna have a good time today—and she'll be back soon. I can see it in her shining face." He winks.

I'm smiling and shaking my head no, but I can't break from his eyes, more brilliant than his jumpsuit. Neil puts out his hand for a high five and I give it some energy. "Time to hit the sky," he booms.

Tom takes me around to meet a few of the other jumpmasters, and Neil follows, shooting all the way. I hope I don't look scared to death. It will be good to have the video. I can watch Tom whenever I want. I'll need to get a VCR.

Tom slides into the plane first and takes my hand to pull me between his legs on the floor. There aren't any seats except for two in front. I can feel his breath warm on my neck and his arms at my sides. The sensuousness of it nearly overcomes the fear, the intimate space and heightened emotion. I know Tom's aware of my feelings. He's done this so many times, with so many other women. He runs the seat belt across my thighs and snaps it. Yes, I'm putting my life in his hands. I'm the hostage and he's my captor—it's almost love. Fear fades with his calm consideration and the heat rising inside me.

The couple and their jumpmasters and the three cameramen scoot aboard. Another jumper is firmly situated backward between my thighs, and my knees are almost at my shoulders. I feel secure. There's not enough room in the plane for a nervous gesture. Someone squeezes the last leg inside and shuts the door. We're off, climbing on an angle in seconds.

I can see nothing but bright blue out the window, no perspective. Tom's legs curve around me, and the warmth builds between my back and Tom's chest.

I picture us in the air, my long hair floating in his face. "Should I tie my hair back?"

"Whatever you want."

I get out a scrunchy and bend forward to loop it around the thick handful of hair. I don't want to obscure his vision at a critical moment.

Neil starts filming again, and Tom's doing something behind me, flashing personality for the camera, no doubt, alternating with tender shoulder squeezing. He hooks us together at the shoulders and hips and situates the ripcord on my jumpsuit. In a few minutes, the pilot calls, "Door." Neil opens it. The air has cooled and it pours into the plane, taking away the warm, secure feeling. Tom has unsnapped our seat belt, and I'm thinking that it could be possible to get tangled on it, with all these straps and buckles dripping off us. It's a long belt, and I'm focused on the idea of getting hooked up just outside the door and dangling. Tom must be aware if it, but I point and mention the possibility. He nods, not like I'm crazy, but that it's good I'm so calm as to think of it. I relax—so many times he's lifted his perfect ass out of this plane. Of course he knows every inch of metal and nylon.

The woman of the couple scoots to the door with her instructor. Their cameraman is already waiting on the wing. Video and still cameras are mounted on his helmet. Looking into the blue air, with no ground in sight, I almost expect them to float like on the video, but no, they fall out of sight instantly, gone. The cameraman has jumped from the wing. The husband scoots next—gone.

It's our turn. Neil climbs out on the wing. "Don't count to three when you get out," Tom says. "Just go straight into the lay-out." He motions me to scoot. I don't notice how I get there, but I'm on the edge, in front of him. "Ready?" he asks.

"Okay," I mouth into the loud noise of engine. We lean. A surge of wind, then looseness. I feel upside down. I'm not sure. I can see only blue. Where is Tom? I'm wondering for the longest time, in slow motion, just wondering, no fear. It's a clean, bright blankness, a feeling I never imagined, maybe like death.

The hazy ground appears, and Tom's arms are there beside me. He's still on my back. I feel no sensation of relief, just understanding. The looseness is replaced by the constant impact of air on my cheeks and hands. We're flat out zooming toward the misty landscape. I hear Tom yelling something into my ear. I lift my head, and there's the camera, with Neil under it, grinning. I wave and wag my tongue.

We spin one way, then the other. Tom is doing it somehow. The wind is screaming, cold, powerful, dizzying.

We stop, and I feel Tom's hand tap my side and realize it's time to pull the ripcord. It no longer seems to matter. I could do this all day. He taps again. I yank the short plastic tube—a long pull straight out—and the yellow wire is free in my hand. There's a sudden whoosh and my legs swing out. The wind is quiet. I hear a light flapping and feel pressure in the straps on my inner thighs. It seems that we're hanging on nothing above the world. The pattern of cane fields is beautiful, even the blackened squares amid the greens, the light browns, and, in the distance, the gray-blues of endless Lake Okeechobee, streaks of mist above it.

"How's that?" Tom asks. His voice is soft, sexy.

I nod. Too much for comment.

"I thought I'd better not spin you too hard. We call that the 'vomitron.' I wasn't sure if I'd like what you had for lunch." He laughs.

I realize that anything I brought up would have been flung right into his face. I can't quite laugh along.

Tom places my hands on the straps on my chest. "Hold on. Let me loosen these leg straps so you're more comfortable."

I hadn't noticed discomfort, but as his fingers loosen the straps that hold up my thighs, I'm totally relaxed—his willing hostage again.

"Want to play?" Tom asks. Before I can guess at what, he pulls the lines down with one arm and we whip fast into a turn. My stomach leaps. "Whoa!" I yell.

He stops immediately. I feel his hand smoothing my hair. It's come loose. We drift in silence. I watch the ground getting closer.

"Remember, all you have to do is lift your legs as we touch down. I'll do all the work."

I nod. I'm back in the trance.

We drift. I see cows and sheep below, endless fields neatly divided by canals. Coming into the airport, we cross a runway. The world is real. "Time to flare," he tells me. "Get ready to raise your feet."

The ground rises fast. Within house height of the grass, he pulls the lines down on each side of me. We halt. He steps into soft gravel. The chute ruffles and falls. We're standing.

He puts a quick kiss on my neck before Neil gets to us. I hope the kiss is on film. "How was it?"

"Great" is all I can say. "Great." I try to step forward to keep from leaning back against him, but the straps are still hooked. I jerk and he steadies me. Neil is filming. "Hang on," Tom says. "She's trying to run away."

He's wrong. I'm not. He unhooks the straps and Neil gives me a high five and motions us over to stand with the couple and their instructors and cameramen. Tom finishes gathering up the chute, and we all stand together, first-timers with our arms up in victory. It's a taste of life I've never known. I'm not the same person I was before I soared like a bird. I like the new me.

WE GO BACK TO THE MANIFEST
building to wait for the video, and Tom brings out a cooler from
behind the counter. He motions me to follow him to a table in the
next room. "I knew you'd be hungry, so I brought a snack. I have a
couple more tandems yet." He has crab and shrimp salad on crusty
rolls, gourmet vegetable chips, also a creamy key lime pie. He
hands me a can of sparkling water and smooths a blue-checkered
cloth napkin on my lap, his long fingers strong on my thighs.

I'm amazed at the attention. I look at the food and wonder how
we'll fit dinner. " 'Too much of a good thing is wonderful'—Mae
West," I tell him.

"You're something else with the quotes."

"Really! What a spread," I say. "Martha Stewart goes on a picnic."

He shrugs. "I know where to shop."

I take a bite of a sandwich. "In Clewiston?"

He shakes his head. "I have my sources."

I'm halfway through my sandwich when Neil comes walking
over. He hands me a tape. "Great jump. Thinking of doing AFF
training?"

I swallow the bite. "I don't know, but I sure enjoyed it. I knew
Tom would take care of me."

"Yeah, he'll do that."

Tom pushes back his chair and stands up. "I've got another

tandem in a minute." He motions to Neil. "Would you mind setting up her video?"

"No problem," Neil says. He motions me toward the TV.

"Be right there," I tell him. I crumble my trash and look for the can.

Neil walks ahead. Tom turns to me. "Sorry to keep you hanging around. I had a feeling this would be a long day. You're going to wait, right?"

"Oh, yeah. If you're not too worn-out." I laugh.

"Not a chance. It'll be awhile, though." He says quietly, "Why don't you go on home and I'll head over there—work up another appetite." He raises his eyebrows a couple times.

I'm taken aback at his suggestion. My place is a mess and much farther away. "I'd rather," he says, when I hesitate.

"Okay. I guess."

"Great. Be there as soon as I can." He turns and heads out the glass door.

I feel a little pissed, wondering if he's lost interest in me and now has other plans. But I'm confused after all the trouble to romance me with the snack.

Neil is waiting for me, and I settle on the leather couch to watch my video. "Enjoy," he says. He hands me a roll of 35-mm shots to get developed. "Catch you later."

Rock music blares and takes my attention to the screen. Tom leaves my mind. There's a twirl of colorful parachutes and signs—fancy editing. The camera zooms in on Tom helping me put on the yellow jumpsuit. My dark hair catches glints of sun streaming into the hangar and my face is beaming. I'm gazing into Tom's eyes too attentively. The camera roams. Neil has captured the atmosphere of the place, a girl in a bikini packing her rig, a huge sleeping dog, the plane against wide-open space.

I wonder who Tom is hooking up with for the next tandem. Maybe he met somebody new during the afternoon, and that's why he's blowing off our plans. It's ridiculous even to think about having any kind of connection with somebody like him.

I focus on the video as the plane starts climbing, feel a surge of excitement that wipes out my uncomfortable feelings. Out we go and backward into a somersault. That explains it. I'd almost forgotten the weird feeling. I laugh. There's a smile on my face all the way around. I shine in my rippling yellow jumpsuit. I feel the excitement rush through my chest as I watch. I can barely breathe.

All the way home, I replay the jump in my mind, making the ride seem fast. I get in the shower, and it feels good, but I start to think about the evening. Something is slightly off. I have an intuition that Tom changed the plan because of something he didn't want to mention. Why would he want to come all the way to my place when his trailer is so close to the airport? If he stands me up, I certainly won't see him again. I can forget all this crap that takes my mind off work.

At 9:30, it's been dark over an hour, and I'm sure he's not coming. I'm ready to strip off my nice pants and blouse and get into pajamas. On the way to the bedroom, I stop in the kitchen to give each dog a carrot. They've already eaten, but they didn't have their vegetable. When they see me open the refrigerator drawer, both of them sit up and put their paws out. "Easy. Easy," I say. I hold a carrot in each hand. Their wet mouths clamp gently. They're sweet, well-trained animals, nice fur-people to have around. Always dependable. Not like tomcats.

I hear his truck. His precise timing again. If I'd have been in my pajamas, I would have told him to go.

I hear his steps on the walk. The dogs leap up, barking—finally. They've missed their cue with all the munching. I suck in a breath. I feel my heart beating in the seconds it takes until he knocks. I push Clue aside and get the door open a foot. Angel sticks her head out, and I pull her back by the collar. A mixed bouquet of pinks and purples passes through the opening. I take them from his fingers and set them on the table. I'm impressed.

"Can I come in?" he calls.

"Yes. That's why I've got the door open." I smile despite myself. I wedge my body in front of the dogs. "Back, back." I pull the door wider and Tom steps in. My breath catches. He's better-looking every time I see him.

The kids stop barking and start sniffing around his legs. He bends and pets them. "I've got treats. Is that okay?" He pulls a pack of meat chews out of his pocket.

I nod. "You sure know what side your bread's buttered on."

Clue and Angel sit immediately. Tom opens the package and feeds them the jerky strips one by one. Their waggling butts can barely stay on the floor.

He hands out the last piece and throws the empty bag on the table.

"You made a hit," I say.

He takes my face in his hands and tilts it up to his mouth. The dogs are trying to push between us, but he wraps his arms around me and I lose focus on anything else. His fingers work down my buttons and his warm hands go inside my bra. I wonder what took him so long to get here, but it doesn't matter anymore.

We step around the dogs and move swiftly to the bedroom. When he gets my pants off and slides inside me, my mind goes into the blue. I'm floating down again, 120-mph winds pushing through my body, divine pressure, the sweet meltdown over and over as his cock drives and my head swirls. I can't take any more, and he's never going to stop. I gasp. I want it to go on and on. It does. There's nothing but his body overpowering mine in the rocking, sweltering blackness. All my senses are concentrated on the friction deep between my thighs and the seal of skin against skin that makes us one hot-breathing, sweating mass. The impossible happens and his cock gets harder. He lets out a long, light groan that sends the last tingling wave rushing over me. He settles down and I fall into a solid stillness as calm as death. I'm wrapped in cotton, wondering if I had a stroke, not caring.

When my mind focuses, I think about all the work I have to do during the week, all the time I'll be doing other things than this, the things that are most important in my life, and I can't remember why they're so important. Tom's snoring lightly at my side, and it doesn't bother me that I like it.

I open my eyes in the dark and gradually make out Clue and Angel on the bed beside me. They're awake, panting. I hear an engine start up and the crunch of gravel. It must have been Tom shutting the door that woke me. I glance at the digital clock—not even midnight. He's got somewhere to go. I feel the dull twinge of distance being kept between us, but I'm too tired to wake up and worry. I can do that in the morning.

I WAKE UP IN A TERRIBLE GLOOM at dawn, knowing I have a long day and a long week ahead. I've never felt this way about work before. Now I know it's not just the sex. I can't deny I have feelings for him. I'm threatened by them. I have no idea where he stands. If I had tears, I might indulge myself in a cry, but I was born without ducts, dependent on tears in a bottle. A squirt of artificial tears doesn't have the same effect—no release, no cleansing from inside. It's a frustration I've always lived with, but at the same time, there's strength that comes from not giving in to useless emotions.

Midmorning, I'm sexing an iguana for a woman, and Corey brings in a big blooming purple orchid. She sets it on the counter and winks. I peer into the iguana's vent and apply pressure against the base of the tail, but I have a hard time keeping my eyes off the plant, where I can see a card on a pick. The iguana squirms and its hemipenes pops through the slit in the skin. "Male. I thought so," I tell the lady. "Be sure you separate the breeding pair from this guy. He'll become aggressive in season."

"I guess I should've gotten two females."

I nod, not really thinking. I turn him back over on his stomach. He claws the table and his feet slide as I hold him in place. "He's a good guy. Just get him his own cage."

I can barely wait to get the reptile back into his carrier and the woman out the door. I snatch the card. It's written front and back. He says to forgive him for leaving so early—we both needed our sleep. He wants to make me dinner at his trailer. The cub misses me, he says. It's signed "Tom." No *love* or *sincerely*, but there's really no room. I imagine him relaying this whole message to the florist. They're probably used to his apologies to women.

His comeback is good, always the unexpected, which I can't resist. The card has his phone number. I call to leave a message. It's a beeper, so I punch in my number.

I should have known he wouldn't give me his home number. Too accessible. I picture him soaring ten thousand feet with his beeper going off, some woman attached to him. Of course, he couldn't hear it. If he doesn't call back soon, I'll have to leave for the park. I put a fecal slide under the microscope and feel irritated at myself for thinking of nothing but Tom and his body and a wild evening in the woods. I forbid myself to worry. I'll get to know Tom and his faults soon enough, and my daydreams will give way to good common sense and self-discipline as always. He rings and I tell him I'll be there at eight.

I rush home and get a shower and arrive at Tom's trailer by quarter till, a little early, so I hope it's okay. I pull up and park. A light's on inside at the far end. I knock and wait, but he doesn't come. I turn the knob and go in. I guess he doesn't need to lock. Who would think somebody lived back here? I hear him talking as I step inside. He's on the phone in the bedroom, it seems. I call, "Tom, I'm here," but he doesn't answer. He's talking loud, setting somebody straight about a mix-up that wasn't his fault. I'm wondering if it's a woman he's talking to. Something about his tone, authoritative, yet careful, makes me think so. I back up and close the door. I'll take a look at the cub so I don't eavesdrop. To listen would mean I cared.

I walk out to the cage. There's enough moonlight to follow the sand path, but the hanging roots and foliage are difficult to avoid. I watch for spiders. This is spider country if I ever saw it. I push some vines out of the way and brush a web from my ear. There's the cage. The cub is in the corner, curled up. I slip the latch and go inside. He's snoring lightly. I walk over quietly and squat down so I can look him over in the filtered moonlight. There's something strange. I stare at the markings on his head. I don't think it's the same cub. It's weird. It has to be Jeepers. I glance around. There's only one cage and I'm in it. Tom couldn't be starting a zoo out here.

I pet the soft fur on the head and his eyes open. He looks at me and yawns. I take a hold of his jaw as he closes it and open it back up. This cub is younger. I've checked over a couple cubs in the last few weeks, so I could be confused, but why would I even think of it? A chill runs like lightning down my spine. I stand up quickly and move out of the cage.

I rush back to the clearing and wipe the mist of sweat off my forehead. I don't know whether I should ask Tom about the cub. Maybe I'm crazy. What sense does it make?

I see the glowing tip of a cigarette moving back and forth in front of the trailer as I approach. Tom's voice comes softly through the darkness. "I saw your car out here. Wondered if you'd traipsed off into the Everglades." He crushes out the cigarette on the gravel drive, moves forward, and puts his hands on my shoulders. He looks into my eyes.

I look down at the few remaining sparks. "I didn't know you smoked."

"One a day, just so I'm not too perfect." He grins. He kisses my forehead. "How are you today?"

"Fine."

"Are you happy to see me?"

I nod. My breath catches.

"I'm happy to see you." He takes my hand and presses it against his jeans into his solid cock. My jaw goes slack as he bends and nuzzles my neck. He pushes my shirt aside and moves his mouth along my collarbone. His arm goes around my back to hold me against him.

As he leads me to the door and opens it, I'm thinking about the cub again. It must be the same cub or Tom would have said something. He knows I saw it.

It's chilly in the trailer. The air is on full blast. A short step and we're in the bedroom, which is nothing but bed with a foot of space on each side.

"Start without me," Tom says. "I need to brush my teeth." He goes into the bathroom.

As I unbutton my shirt, I wonder at how quickly I've gotten to this point again without a thought. Am I that desperate? I notice how prettily the room is decorated, despite the cheap wood paneling and built-in squareness of the bed and nightstands. Blue curtains that match a country quilt show more attention paid than I would have expected. He comes back, and I stop caring about the room. He lifts my arms over my head and my shirt slides off backward. I'm lost to his mouth in my armpit, moving down my ribs, warming up the room, making my nipples taut. He sits down on the bed and pulls me onto his lap like a kid, then starts kissing and caressing my forehead and temples. I have no desire to resist him. He gets a finger in my ear and pulls a little downward, stretching the limits of relaxation almost to pain. He certainly knows the tricks. I don't care what cub's out there in the cage. I go with my body and forget everything else.

When he's finished with me, I feel myself sunk deep into the mattress. My head swirls like I'm drunk and a crazed thought runs through it that this man is the devil. I look at his arm across my tits. He's made a study, done his homework on female anatomy. I'm dazed. I wonder if he'll want to get rid of me in a few minutes and I'll have to try to drive home. I pull up the sheet.

I wake to the smell of garlic and sounds of movement from the kitchen. My stomach growls. I remember we haven't had dinner. I slip on my shirt and do a few buttons, squirt some tears into my eyes. I wander into the small kitchen. My crotch is wet and I can feel the lips rubbing between my legs, swollen and slightly sore, extrasensitive. Tom turns from the stove as I yawn. He's wearing a white terry-cloth robe, which is hanging open, a striking contrast to his golden-haired chest and the shadowy landscape below.

"Sleepy baby," he says. "You didn't need to get up. I was going to surprise you."

"You did."

I see fish searing in a pan. He brings me a glass of wine. I take a sip and my face puckers. "It's good. My mouth's just not awake."

"We'll fix that," he says.

He bends to kiss me, and I reach inside his robe to the warmth. He rubs against me, ready to go again. I'm ready, too, in a sexual haze. I wrap my fingers around the warm silk of his cock. My mouth wants to go there, saliva welling, but he takes the wine from my hand and draws me to his mouth. I put my arms around his neck and feel the warmth intense in my chest. I don't remember ever having this feeling before.

He pulls back and tilts his head to give me a soft glance. "Let's eat so we can keep up our strength." He kisses my cheek and turns toward the stove. Already I don't want to give this up. I don't want to think about anything else.

I WAKE UP AT SEVEN, DAYLIGHT, AS usual. I had planned to ask Tom to set the alarm for five. I know the dogs are in agony, and I still have nearly an hour's drive. Tom is angelic in sleep, with the hair spread across his forehead and long golden lashes against his tan cheeks. He's curled on his side, cozy as a cat. I kiss his freckled shoulder and he opens his eyes. Their blue hits me and I take in air. I've never been with a man this beautiful. "Didn't mean to wake you," I say. I can't take my eyes off him.

"S'okay. I'm not awake." His eyes close again, and with the magnetism broken, I'm able to stretch and roll myself out on the other side. I pick up my clothes from the bottom of the bed and the floor and grab my bag and take them into the bathroom. I shut the door and let go like a faucet. I can feel my labia, swollen and warm from the long workout. My whole body's alive.

If it wasn't for the dogs, I'd crawl under the covers and give Tom a little wake-up. But I have to hurry. I find my toothbrush in the bottom of my purse but can't locate any toothpaste. I open the medicine cabinet—nearly empty, no toothpaste. He isn't big on drugs. There are two drawers, but I hesitate to look in Tom's stuff. I take a quick peek in the top one. Good. Crest.

I'm putting it back, when I notice a piece of jewelry in the corner. I close the drawer. I open it. I pick up a gold earring, a tiny loop with delicate scrolling, expensive. Tom doesn't have a pierced ear—I don't think. Anyway, it's a woman's. I drop the loop back and do my teeth and splash off my face. It isn't anything I can ask about—Oh, Tom, why do you have an earring in your drawer? It could have been there for years, an old girlfriend's, maybe even the tenant before him. Maybe somebody else he's dating. Not my business at this point. I dab on some makeup and gather my stuff.

Tom is sound asleep on his right side, no earring hole on the left. I kiss his neck, and he mumbles without opening his eyes and reaches a hand out.

"Don't get up. I have to rush."

"I'll call you, hon."

The drive seems to take forever, but finally I get home, and it's still there, same old, same old. I open the door and see that somebody's peed in the kitchen, but I don't care. The kids are waggling around, and I feel good. I take them out for their walk in the cool air. My pants rub between my legs, and I call up an instant rush of Tom—a physical memory—inside me. It's a wonderful feeling, warmth beyond the sex. Then I start thinking about that fucking new cub. I wish I had asked him.

I get to Lion Country at noon. It's my half day there. There's a note for me from Gerald Path, the full-time vet. He's out on the lion veldt and wants me to catch up with him. It strikes me as odd, because I have a slew of inoculations due. Must be something important.

I get the little Jeep and head over. It's starting to drizzle, and I'm beginning to feel a little down in the stickiness and the long day ahead. What could Tom's explanation for the cub possibly be?

Gerald flags me down at one of the fences. I park and walk over.

"I just got a report this morning. The last batch of feline leukemia vaccine might not have been any good—a production problem. We need to revaccinate all seven lion cubs with their last dose. I haven't had a chance to get to it."

"No problem. I'll do it now."

"Thanks. I checked, and we're just within the time limit, so we don't have to start over."

I go back to the Care Center to get the vaccine. I realize I should call Tom and tell him I need to vaccinate Jeepers with the new serum. It's a good reason to go back over and see him again right away. It'll give me a chance to look at the cub in better light and find out if I was mistaken or get the truth so I can quit fretting. We can spend the evening in bed.

I beep him from the park hospital and do paperwork for nearly an hour, and he still hasn't called back. I beep again and give it another twenty minutes. In midweek I wouldn't think he'd be so busy. Of course, he wouldn't recognize the number, maybe thinks it's somebody soliciting.

By late afternoon, I still haven't gotten a callback. I'm not the kind of person who just drops in, but I get in my car and head his way. It'll be dark if I don't. It's Tom's fault he hasn't given me a regular phone number. If he's not there, I'll just go back to the cage by myself.

AS I TURN ONTO THE UNPAVED road to his trailer, another car meets me coming out. The woman driving looks annoyed. She has to wait while I back up so she can pass. She's in a Mercedes—one of the few I've seen out here in the country. The thought that she could be coming from Tom's house sends an icy sting straight to my bones. I pull myself together. I have no idea where that road goes after it passes the driveway to his trailer. Any number of people could live beyond his piece of jungle.

I pull up in front and am surprised to see Tom's car. He probably tried to reach me as soon as I left. I glance at my hair in the rearview mirror and open the car door. Tom pops open the trailer door, looking startled. He's already by my side as I close the car door, and he gives me a peck.

"Am I catching you at a bad time? Sorry, I was—"

"I just now had a chance to call you. I got your machine."

I tell him about the serum. It feels like a cheap excuse at this point.

He tells me to go ahead out to the cage. He'll be right there.

I set out on the path, noticing the beauty of the vegetation in the last rays of sun. It's like the first evening I came out here—when I wanted nothing to do with Tom, or so I'd told myself.

No spiders in sight. I come up to the clearing. There's Jeepers asleep in his usual spot. Yes, it does look like Jeepers, the way I first saw him with his belly against the fountain.

"Shame to wake him up."

I look over my shoulder. Tom is standing behind me on the path. He looks fuckable, with his sunglasses on and shirt half-unbuttoned.

I walk in the cage and set my bag down, get out my stethoscope to start the examination. I crouch and look at the markings on the cub's head.

"He's growing like a weed, huh?" Tom asks.

"Yeah, sure is." I'm thinking, Yeah, shrank, then grew. I open his mouth. More teeth than two days ago. I know I'm not crazy. If this isn't the first Jeepers, it's a third one.

"Been feeding him well. Just what you told me."

I put the stethoscope to the cub's back, then chest, look him over further. I can feel my own heart beating almost as fast as his. I get out the syringe I've prepared with one cc of feline leukemia vaccine. I don't know what else to do. I can't even guess what kind of scam is going on. Tom holds Jeepers while I plunge the needle into the skin between the shoulders.

We walk back to the trailer. Tom takes my hand and I hold on, wanting to say something but not knowing where to start. I have to think it out, find the right question to get the truth without accusing him of something.

He stops by my car and takes me close and kisses me hard. He leans against me until I'm pushed back against the door with the pressure of his body. His hard cock grinds against my hip and his mouth works down the sensitive surface of my throat. He straightens and moves back to look me up and down. He tilts my chin with a fingertip. I feel vulnerable looking into his eyes, like I'm the one hiding something.

"You're tense. Everything okay?"

"I . . . Rough day."

"Poor baby," he says. He smooths back my hair. "I guess you want to get home and get some rest."

His tone relaxes me instantly. I put my finger on his cheek, run it down his neck. "I'm not in that big a hurry."

"Oh?"

"Unless you want to get rid of me."

"Not at all." He moves close again and puts his arm around my waist. "Not at all, sweetheart."

I look at him. My mind is fastened on the cub again.

"In that case, I have something here to help relax you."

He opens the trailer door and pulls me in behind him. He takes me onto the couch and tucks a pillow under my head.

"Close your eyes," he says.

I feel one shoe and sock come off and then the other. He massages the ball of my right foot, then puts his fingers between the toes. Again, I put off thinking about lion cubs. I'm weak, and he knows exactly how to make my brain shut down. He rubs up and down the outside of my big toe, pressure somewhere between pain and ecstasy. He does the same with the Achilles tendon. He strips off my pants and panties, and the cool air makes me tingle with need. He moves up my calves, squeezing the muscles in his hard hands, then up the insides of my thighs, one at a time, hands massaging, until he parts my legs, dips his face, and follows with his warm, wet mouth. His hot, strong tongue takes me right out of this world. I'm trembling and breathing hard in seconds and I come fast. He's kneeling on the floor and he rests his head on my vulva and snuggles his arms over my hips; his hands cup my tits under the shirt. "Relax," he says.

I try to doze in the warm feeling, but I can't. I stroke his temple down to the jaw. He raises his head. "Feel better?"

"It's a start," I tell him, and wink.

He stands and pulls his pants down, and his cock springs out.

"You're always a step ahead, aren't you?" I say.

"Two steps. How 'bout you turn over on your hands and knees for me."

I keep contact with his eyes and unbutton my shirt and slip it off. He seems distracted somehow. I get down on the carpet, positioning my body for the deep penetration as he takes my hips from behind and slides inside me hard and hot until I moan and climax. He continues to pump into me. We collapse.

When I have my breath, I get up off the floor. Tom's eyes are closed. I go into the bathroom and sit down on the toilet. I know I have to pull myself together and go home. I have to break from him long enough to restart my brain and think things out. I can't do that lying next to him. I have an early-starting, long day tomorrow.

I reach for the toilet paper. The roll is empty. I open the cabinet under the sink. There's the package with a box of Tampax beside it. A wave of heat comes over me. The box isn't old. I recognize the recent label. I stand and open the medicine cabinet. It was nearly empty before. Now there's moisturizer, liquid face soap, mud mask, organic deodorant. I can't hold back my anger at being played as the only one. I close both doors and walk into the living room. Tom is on his back on the couch, eyes closed.

"You have a bathroom full of women's cosmetics."

His eyes blink open.

"Whose are they? Or is it a collection? I guess you're the drop-zone stud and I'm just the bunny du jour."

His mouth is slightly open.

"I should have known it." I gather my clothes into a pile on the coffee table and step into my panties. His eyes are on my crotch, like he's watching dessert get put away before his second helping.

"No. I'm sorry—very sorry. I know I should have told you about this. . . ."

"You would have missed out on a piece of ass if you had."

"C'mon. I'm no playboy. Sit down and listen to me. I'm sorry." He takes my hand. I'm limp enough that I let myself slump next to him on the couch.

"Those are my wife's things—we're separated. She left that stuff there three months ago and I just didn't bother to return it. That's all."

By this time, I don't care if he thinks I'm a snoop. "It wasn't in there last time I was here."

"I stashed it. I admit it. I didn't want to talk about it. It doesn't mean anything—really."

"Why'd you put it back?"

"I'd thrown it all in my underwear drawer. I just put it back in the cabinet instead of sorting it out. I forgot about it."

I shake my head. "What's there to sort? Huh? I don't believe you. I'm not going to be the 'other woman.' "

"It's true. Think about it. I took you to meet all my friends. Introduced you. Would I do that?"

"I have no idea." I'm trying to think if he showed any affection in front of other people. I remember the lunch, probably not something he'd do for a casual friend.

"I was ready to tell you . . . just waiting for a good time."

"When would that be?"

"I didn't want to scare you off. You were tough enough. . . ."

My stomach has a knife blade running through it. This is bullshit and I've known it all along. I finish dressing quickly.

"I'm not letting you run off," Tom says.

I shake my head. "I don't know what you're trying to put over on me."

"Nothing. I swear. I didn't want to take a chance." He bows his head and puts his hand to his forehead. He exhales heavily.

I put my hand on my hip. "What?"

He looks at me, eyes wide. "I love you."

I shake my head, incredulous.

"I love you, Des. Does that make any difference?" I don't move, and he pulls me closer and pushes my head down on his shoulder.

He takes a deep breath. "Don't worry, sweetheart. She's long gone. I'll throw that stuff away, like I should have already."

I don't believe it, not at all. But I want to. I let him crush me to his chest and press my face with his palm. I'm helpless between him and the warmth I feel coming out of me. "Fuck," I say softly, feeling every letter of the word. I don't have the strength to ask any more questions. His mouth moves down and mine moves up. "Fuck."

His lips cover mine, then slowly slide off. "You're already mine and you know it. We're hooked on each other."

Something about the word *hooked* sends a slant of light to my brain and gives me the motivation to unwrap myself from his arms. He's hit on it. I am hooked, and I don't like the dangling feeling. I'm being pulled his way, regardless of the importance of my own life. I'm not up to slinking around, draining my energy in a tug-of-war with some other unsuspecting woman. "I better go," I tell him. I open my mouth to add something more forceful, but nothing comes out and I close it again.

Tom lets his shoulders slump, resigned, so quickly. No more explanations or arguments. I grab my purse and walk slowly out the door, knowing it's best never to see him again, but giving him all the time possible to call me back before I get into the car, in case there's some other convincing information. No sound from inside. I drive off, wondering if I've made an awful mistake.

ON THE DRIVE HOME, I FEEL MY face tightening into knots—and the burning sensation of tears I don't have that want to come. My stomach is a chunk of granite. Two weeks earlier, I would have told him to shove it and never looked back. Now I'm in pain and actually considering whether what he said can be the truth. I run a possible scene through my brain: Tom's beeper going off when I called, his glancing and putting it back in his pocket, throwing his wife a name she'll recognize, no chance for him to call me, no time to move her stuff out of the bathroom. Fuck. It makes so much sense. No wonder he never gave me the phone number.

I'm not happy when I get into bed. Despite my battered psyche, remembering his touch calls a rush of passion, chills of pleasure through my body. I should have asked more questions, given him half a chance. It takes me a long time to get to sleep. I'm angry with both of us.

As I shower and dress in the morning, I can't stop trying to figure out if he's telling me the truth, if they're really split. There's a leaden feeling in my chest that I know as resignation, my body ahead of my mind, set on what I'm going to do regardless. He's told a lie that weighs on me like a cement block, yet I'll keep seeing him, if it isn't too late—if I haven't already pushed him back to her. Clearly, I'm making a wrong choice, but only kidding myself to think I could stop seeing him through willpower. I make a mental list, the pro's on one side—namely, his body; his company—the con's on the other—the lie, the cub, and a long list of why I'm better without him for myself and my profession. There's no sense in tedious pondering about the truth of his words, because I know only what he's told me, and he's told me only what he wanted to.

I wring my brain for memories of the day of my tandem, trying to figure out if he treated me like a lover or an acquaintance in front of his friends. There's nothing I can recall. It would be early to show a lot of affection in public.

By the time I get into the office, there's already a message. Tommy's voice, sweeter than the thousands of acres of sugar outside. "I love you, Desi. There's nobody can compete with you. You're the best—we're made for each other. It's—supernatural. Nothing's gonna keep us apart."

I recognize words from a song. Fuck. I guess everything that's true about love has already been said a million times. It's the feeling washing over my body and pushing me down on the chair like negative g's that counts, my halted breathing when I hear his voice. He couldn't be seeing his wife on a regular basis. What could he tell her on the nights he's been at my place, the Saturday night I spent with him?

I listen to my other messages and do my callbacks. I'm looking out the front window from the desk and I can see the endless fields of sugarcane being cut and gathered beyond the row of royal palms across Bacom Point Road, so desolate for a human—so deadly for the rabbits, rats, raccoons, and snakes when the burns rip across the fields with the wind. I remember how I found it peaceful when I came to look around, an escape from all the sorority and fraternity crap over the past years.

How lucky I felt to find this place—the old vet ready to retire after heart surgery, a price I could afford to borrow. I was ecstatic when I got the loan—instantly a country doctor, such a tranquil, civilized occupation. Screw it. Nothing but sky and stalks, as vast as Midwest farmland, as hot as hell.

In six months, I haven't met any single women—no one to confide in—not to mention no single men. Even Corey is only an acquaintance, with her three children and mother to care for. There are the wealthy sugar plantation wives, older women who bring in their small dogs. They're polite, in their separate worlds. Most of the men I see in town are farmers, laborers, and machine operators, and I haven't had the inclination to meet them at the local bar. Maybe if I head east into Palm Beach—but it's intimidating, and there's really no time. I haven't done it.

I pick up the phone and beep Tom. He still hasn't given me his home number. That's the first thing I'm going to ask for.

I'm expressing the anal glands on a schnauzer when the phone rings an hour later. I have no choice but to let the machine take a message. I finish up with a shot of antibiotics and hand the little pooch to his owner. She's barely out the door, and I grab the phone to beep Tom again. I don't know what's the matter with me. Yes, I do.

I finish with my appointments for the day at noon. I turn off the fluorescent lights, lock the front door, and go back to the apartment. I'm starving and haven't got anything besides peanut butter and jelly. I decide to hurry and treat myself to lunch at the Home Cooking restaurant down the road. It's roast turkey day, and mashed potatoes with gravy always help me feel good. I pull off my scrub suit, and I'm getting a clean pair of shorts and a shirt out of the dryer when Clue and Angel start going nuts and race to the side door.

I follow them to take a peek out the window. It's Tom. He's detouring around a fresh land mine that Clue dropped this morning in the middle of the walkway. I'm standing there in my bra and panties and socks. If I don't put on clothes, my surrender is already

decided. I step around the dogs and open the door. They stop barking and start to wag. Tom's eyes gleam and his mouth moves
slowly into a wide smile. His look sweeps down my frame, lingers
on the sturdy bra. I smile back, helpless.

"You've been waiting for me," he says.

Sex rushes over me. I reach down and push the dogs back, not
taking my eyes off his face. He comes in and sets a bag on the
counter.

"Brought a lunch. Thought I'd just take a chance that you'd
have time to eat."

"Barely," I whisper.

Tom starts unbuttoning his shirt, and I reach back and undo
my bra, let those babies out, what they're already dying for—
regardless that it's been less than twenty-four hours.

"It's only sandwiches and chips."

I slip off my panties. "I'll eat mine in the car."

He drops his jeans on the floor. They're black and I'm thinking,
Dog hair city, but he moves forward and takes me, rubs his thumbs
over the nipples that have budded. My thoughts are gone. I step
into him with my arms around his neck, and our mouths come
together on their own. We shuffle through the dogs to the bedroom, where he lays me out and slides that hard, smooth cock
tight inside my lubricated grip. The magic works fast—we're in
good practice. A blush blooms across my chest as I melt. I don't
blame Tom—whatever he had to do with his wife—we're a perfect
fit. I'm so fucking easy to convince. I might as well give up.

As I drive toward the park, I can still feel the warm swelling of
my genital region and the wetness in my panties that's becoming a
daily event. I chomp into the tuna salad sandwich and feel free and
full of energy, as light as the seed tassels on the miles of sugarcane
floating beside me. I want to have a long talk with Tom and find out
just how long they've been separated and if he's serious about a
divorce. But I won't rush him to do anything he doesn't want to.

TOM STOPS OVER AGAIN IN THE evening, and I let my cares roll off my back, like water off a tortoise shell. He's got time to spend with me, and he's willing to fit it into my schedule. Without my saying anything, he tells me he's going ahead with the divorce. I say there's no rush, but can't keep the beaming smile off my face. He doesn't stay over. He's right—it's better for both of us in many ways. I let it go.

Over the next month, I lose some of the tension. We become more than an incredible fit. A smile takes over my face every time Tom turns up. I never had this combination of friend and lover before. He stops by during the week sometimes for lunch and fixes a few things around the office. He's handy and likes to do repairs. He enjoys walking the dogs when I run short on time, sometimes driving them to the drop zone to spend the afternoon where they can run loose. Bear is the official DZ dog, a big brown rug of a fellow, and there's Lucky, the terrier, and Cubby, the German short-haired pointer. They all play together, running among the groups practicing dirt dives, the dogs having as much fun as the skydivers.

It isn't long before I'm tired of hearing about all the fun—I want to be there with Tom, adding this new thrill to my life. Toward the end of the month, I decide it's time for me to start my training for the accelerated free fall certification. I want to jump into the wild blue yonder on my own, fly and land myself, uncontrolled by anyone else's skill. I want to test my spirit, find out what

I'm made of, fit into the select group called skydivers, Tom's group of true friends. I can't think of a better life.

I can arrange to keep my Saturday afternoons free by putting in an extra hour on a few other days. I have a housekeeper to clean the office once a week, and she agrees to do the apartment for thirty dollars. I can go a little easier on myself and still not interfere with work.

I plan to do a half-day training the next Saturday and finish the six to eight hours on Sunday for the initial jump. On Friday, Tom invites me to spend Saturday night at the trailer, instead of making the drive back and forth from home. I meant to ask him all week. Now that he brings up the idea, I realize it was the fear he'd say no that stopped me from saying anything. I haven't seen or heard more about his wife, but I haven't asked. She's easy to block out, since Tom lives freely and never uses her name. I figure she has her own life, and the marriage piece of paper is so inconsequential to both of them, they just haven't bothered to do the legal details of divorcing. There's no reason to push. Marriage is an abstract idea. I'm not ready for it myself, maybe never will be. The word *wife* balls my stomach into a fist, an inherited condition from my mother, who never married my father. Aside from the occasional embarrassment at a young age, I saw she'd made a good choice. They've spent some happy years together, with a few months off here and there. She's always had her own interests, like roach collecting along the Amazon or platypus measuring in Australia. Now she has Daddy cooking at her health-food café in Cincinnati. It keeps her young, having freedom.

I'm buzzed on my way to the DZ Saturday afternoon. I feel an unusual clarity. I look at the cane and the bright road ahead, light smoke from a burning field in the distance. I see contrast, texture, color. I smell orange blossoms from miles away. The seed tassels ripple and wave, as if they're dancing to the music on my car radio. I realize it's the everyday landscape, shaped into a vision of ecstasy by my brain on adrenaline. This is my brain on drugs—naturally occurring substances. If I drop to earth today, a thud on the grass, ending all my hard work and ambitions, follow Grandma into the light, oh well. It could be worse. I've accomplished all my goals, and it's not the perfect life I expected anyway. A fast demise is almost comforting, no more stress, a proud way to die—an easy choice compared to a traffic accident, a stroke, or a long, painful bout of cancer. But I'd much rather live. For skydiving—and Tom.

It's hard to keep my foot light on the pedal with the long, straight road ahead. I'm wildly energized. There are still hours of training and a night with Tom between me and the giant leap. The classroom has always been a place of excitement for me, and tests are my favorite part. This will be the test of all time.

As I park, Tom is packing a parachute in front of the manifest building. I walk toward him. The bright rainbow of nylon is splashed out on the grass, and he's walking forward, pulling up the lines to straighten them. The combination of bright colors, blue sky, and his body are almost too much to bear. He's wearing that shining white jumpsuit, almost skintight. The aqua trim makes a U-turn across the top of his buttocks, bringing out his tapered waist and classically sculpted cheeks. I realize the air is a little cooler today. There's been a sudden drop in humidity, a slight breeze, which I hope means cooler weather is coming. I'd be sweating in that suit, but he looks comfortable, cool—in every sense of the word.

I walk up and step to his side to watch him.

He catches me in his peripheral vision. "Hey, sweetheart."

By now, I enjoy his terms of affection. I kiss him on the cheek, looking around, wondering if it matters. He doesn't flinch. He bends to gather up the chute and hangs it across his shoulder. He reaches inside the bundle of nylon and methodically works his arm back and forth. I can't tell what he's doing, but I figure he's good at it.

"Does everybody pack their own?"

"Most people. The main. The reserve can only be packed by a certified rigger, or under the observation of one."

"Sounds good to me."

"I'm a rigger. It's my life—I need to know everything there is about skydiving."

"How often do people use their reserves?"

"One in a thousand jumps is the average, but it has to be repacked every hundred and twenty days—just to be sure it doesn't sit around and rot, or get some critters inside that chew the lines." He bends to grab the fabric underneath and pulls it up to cover the folds, twists the material in back. He flings the whole thing on the floor, crouches next to the perfect cone shape it lands in, and begins to smooth the top layer.

"Yeah," I say. "Roaches the size they grow here will eat anything. Ever happen to anybody you know? I mean the reserve not opening."

He puts his knee on the cone of shiny nylon, bending it into an S and working it into the bag. I can't help but look at his smooth ass and on down the backs of his thighs.

"Double malfunction is almost nonexistent. I've known people that didn't deploy their reserves for one reason or another, or had entanglements, but no bug-eaten canopies."

"How many accidents here?"

"No fatalities. You're better off up there than on the highway."

I hear the soaring I've learned to recognize and turn to the horizon. Seven or eight open canopies are high above the field. Just like birds, they float, gliding toward the target. The canopies are like huge predators, outstretched wings above prey hanging down. One jumper swoops low along the ground and steps lightly to earth. Another makes a swift turn and drops into a tiptoe run, graceful and assured. I'm wondering how to recognize the airport from so far up. "Just on the far-fetched chance the reserve doesn't open—anything else I can do besides . . . bite the dust?"

He shakes his head. "It's a minor possibility you have to accept, no matter what you're doing."

"Follow Grandma into the light, huh?"

Tom laughs. "Fly to Grandma."

"Doesn't sound so bad."

"Much worse ways to go."

I wait while he finishes gathering the lines into bunches and securing each one with a rubber band, stuffing the whole thing into the bottom portion of his container. I have to face it—I'm going to jump out of a plane, relying on cloth, string, Velcro, and rubber bands.

He looks up at me. "There are a few things you have to get right; otherwise, you can stuff it in the bag almost any way and it'll open."

Tom takes me into the manifest building and introduces me to Dolly, who's behind the counter. She gets out another stack of papers for me to sign. I don't bother to read them this time, just skim through, initialing all the empty boxes. I write down my mother's name and address to be contacted in case of emergency.

Tom says Gerson will do my classroom training. I nod, but I'm disappointed. He walks me outside, over to the hangar. "You'll like him fine." He winks. "I don't wanna have to stare at your body for six hours and not do anything with it." He reaches down and gives me a pat on the cheek. "Don't worry. I'll have a grip on you going out of the plane."

We walk in through the side door. There are piles of colorful nylon and lines stretched out all over the concrete. A couple people are packing. We step between the lines and around a group of wood cutouts—foam-padded torso shapes with arms and legs—on rollers. "What are those?" I ask Tom.

"Sex toys."

"What?"

"Creepers—to practice relative work."

"Formations?"

He stops walking and puts his hand on my back. It's only a brotherly gesture, probably a habit with all his students, but I like the feel of it. He goes into teaching voice. "To practice the movements. Relative work is staying relative to one another during freefall. You have to learn to adjust your body vertically and horizontally at the same time. Body position causes you to fall faster or slower and move in whatever direction you want." He turns to me, and I'm caught off guard by those eyes—as always. I feel myself wide-eyed.

"You can start doing two-ways and three-ways when you get comfortable with the solos," he says. "It's kind of a physical chess game—played in a minute. You have to think ahead in all directions, get points, and try not to get taken out—and not take anybody else out, either."

"I'll get comfortable? Relatively speaking, right?"

He ignores my attempt at a joke. "You'll be surprised. Your body learns—then we'll do a nude dive."

I stare harder into those big blues. He can't be serious.

He laughs. "Once you get really good at landing."

"You play chess?" I ask him. I'm thinking there's something we have in common.

He shakes his head. "No—my ex tried to get me into it."

His eyes shift and I know he's reading my face, noticing it would have been better not to bring her up.

"That was a long while back, when we were trying to work things out—find a hobby together. It didn't suit me. I could never fit into her world." He points out Gerson standing in the doorway of a room built into the far side of the hangar. Gerson motions to me. "There you go," Tom says. "I've got to take a tandem. See you later." He squeezes my shoulder.

I nod and smile and he turns and heads out.

I walk toward Gerson. He's a classic, tall and dark, gleaming teeth in a wide smile. I've never seen such a high concentration of good-looking guys. The magic of altitude?

He comes toward me. "Destiny?"

"Yes. I'm your student."

He's got dangerously striking features. "I thought you were going to say that you're my destiny." He winks.

"Part of it." I wink back. Flirtation seems to go naturally with the training.

He motions me into the little classroom. Obviously, they're not into impressive decor. There are two split and worn plastic-covered armchairs, a TV and VCR on an old desk, some straps hanging from the ceiling. Gerson looks at his watch. "Take a seat. If we can get four hours in today, you can make your first jump sometime tomorrow morning."

I have a pad full of notes by six, when I walk back into manifest, looking for Tom. Like everything, there's a lot more involved than what's on the surface. I'm reviewing the malfunction video in my head—high-speed malfunctions, low-speed malfunctions, specifics of what can go wrong so you know whether to try to fix it or cut away and pull the reserve. The landing is not so simple, either. You have to fly a pattern like aircraft, and land into the wind. I'm wondering how I'll recognize the airport and know which direction the wind is blowing. Easy to remember: Stay away from trees and power lines and buildings. Don't fly over anything you don't want to land on. Okay. Flare at ceiling height. Don't land on the runway. How will I judge? Will I have my right mind? There's no way to practice. Unless I have baby bird instinct buried deep in my limbic brain, the world is likely to go on without me.

I pet Bear at the side door and watch a group of six practicing movements almost like a dance—taking one another's hands and shoulders and changing places. They're an extreme mixture of ages and types. One older guy, maybe in his sixties, is shirtless and tattooed over most of his chest and stomach. As he bends to take hold of the edge of a girl's shorts, I see two eyes tattooed on the top of his head. Okay. Anyone can fit in here. I go inside. Dolly points out the window. Tom is on his way down. I dash out the front, but I don't know his canopy colors to pick him out. I watch them one by one, perfect landings, like birds touching down.

Tom comes trudging across the grass, his canopy bundled in his arms. I stand where I am, inside the orange don't-cross line, enjoying the vivid colors against the sunset, watching the last two guys drop in and gather up the yards of nylon. Fear flickers in my mind, now that I know it's not all as simple as it looks. There's one small woman packing right on the field. She's shining in a black patent leather–like jumpsuit, steaming inside it, I imagine. I will soon join this group of fearless humans—or die trying.

I'm wondering if I can give Tom a kiss as he gets close, but he doesn't stop walking, and I pick up my pace to stay beside him.

"Ready to try it?" he asks.

I put out a smile that feels confident, but my voice is quiet. "Tomorrow."

Tom has to go back to the hangar and get packed so he'll be ready for the first load in the morning. I wait and watch the new tandem videos with three women who have just finished. They mention that there's a party that night, a bonfire, and food and beer supplied by one of the skydivers, who's having a birthday. Everyone's invited. I wonder if Tom wants to stay around. I would like to stay for a while, get to know some new people.

As I watch the videos, I see how similar people are, notice the instinctive human behaviors in common. I see the same fear, the amazement, the relief and jubilation back on the ground. I've never liked knowing this, that I'm a near replica of everyone else in feeling and reaction, under the power of things that rule our lives—brain chemistry and environment and, beyond that, chance. I haven't thought about this for a long time. It's the fear of death that makes life so acute—charged and meaningful. It's not a comfortable feeling, but I want to keep it.

I feel Tom put his hand on my shoulder. He stands behind me, looking at the credits on the video—Danovision. I wonder who Dano is.

I look up into Tom's blue eyes. He's got a piece of the sky locked inside each one. I never get tired of them.

The women on the couch take their videos and go. Tom comes around and sits beside me. "Ready to head out?"

I tell him about the party. "Sounds like fun. I'd like to stay a little."

"It'll take an hour before everybody gets organized."

I take his hand. "Do you mind waiting?"

"Not for you, dear."

I can't tell if there's sarcasm there, but he's smiling sweetly. He says to go on outside while he checks something in the video office, that he'll be right back.

I go out to catch a few last rays at the picnic table. I see people gathering by the trailer called DZ Mom's Kitchen. There are two tall spool tables inlaid with tile and covered with skydive graffiti, stools, and a few folding chairs. A pickup truck filled with wood and skydivers backs in and everybody jumps off and starts unloading. Shaggy Bear comes running, out of breath from chasing the truck.

I've been there twenty minutes, and Tom still hasn't come out of the hangar. I walk on over to where the fire is blazing with kindling. The guys are beginning to stand close, even though the air is barely cooled to a temperature below sweating. I lean with my elbows on the spool table and watch the fire.

Dolly comes over and sets down her beer. "Glad you decided to stay for the party. This is a fun group." She points to the men standing in a group close by. "There's Dido, Kelly, Ronnie, Chris, V. J., Patrick, and Jason—you'll get to know everybody. Cal—over there—is an acrobatics pilot. Patrick and Jason are instructors. The others are the Miami boys."

A couple of them glance over. Amazing lookers again—not an average guy among them. They're caught up in a discussion. I hear the words *cutaway* and *entanglement*. There's laughter, joking about the possibility of fatal injury. I turn back to Dolly.

She points over by the beer, "Simon, Glen, Owen, John . . ." The names are rolling through my brain. I wonder what Tom's doing all this time. I'm sure Dolly is feeling obligated to entertain me. "Simon made his hundredth jump today, so he'll probably get pied tonight," Dolly says.

"Pied?"

She brings her hand up flat against her face. "Coconut cream, key lime—or squirted with cans of whipped cream, whatever his friends decide."

"That's a regular thing?"

"One hundred, one thousand, two thousand—"

I'm thinking, I don't have to worry. I'll never get to a hundred. In fact, I never have to worry about anything again—not saving money, not dieting—I'll be following Grandma into the light tomorrow.

"Go get yourself a beer," Dolly says.

I wonder if my face is tense. "Thanks," I tell her. I head over to the tap, watch the amber swirl into the plastic cup, appreciate what might be my last beer.

I walk back through the grass, feeling the slight coolness of the air. It's gotten dark. Looking up, I get a rush from the million stars. "I wonder where Tom is," I say to Dolly. "He said he was coming over in a few minutes."

"Probably returning his wife's call. She left a message in manifest."

I watch a look slip across her face. She's seen the shock on mine and realizes a cat is out of the bag, a big one. We look at each other. I feel the question frozen in my eyes. Her lips are slightly open. I need to ask the details, and she looks ready to tell, but we both hold back. I wonder if she's friends with his wife. "Maybe he's at a safety meeting," she says. We pick up our beers and slug 'em.

Caleb, the owner of Air Adventures, comes over and asks how my training is going. He says I should get a working video tomorrow from Neil so I can see my form. I say, "Okay, good idea," but I'm more focused on thinking of Tom on the phone. Caleb introduces Howard, one of the instructors. He asks about my training and tells me how he comes from a family of skydivers, his father and uncle, who used round chutes, more dangerous, unlike the rectangular canopies we have now, which are safe and easy to land.

I'm nodding and half-listening, divided by this incredible death-defying thing that I'm caught up in and Tom, questions that make me feel so small that I can't dare to jump out of a plane.

Howard tells the story of his first jump years ago. He had no interest, but he had to do it once to satisfy his father. His rig had an old-style ripcord over the shoulder, and he jerked off the whole mechanism when he tried to pull, so he had to wrap the cord halfway around his neck to get the leverage and pull far enough to open the chute. I keep glancing back toward the hangar, phrasing questions for Tom in my mind.

"How did you think to do that?" I ask Howard.

"My mind was perfectly clear. No fear at that point—skydiving became part of my life after that."

He picks up a conversation with another guy and I sit down in a lawn chair by the fire. Where the hell is Tom? The big guy, Owen, is next to me, and he holds out a picture he says is "Groucho." I look close. It's a penis with glasses and black pubic hair like a mustache. A cigar is held where the mouth would be. I chuckle, pretend not to be shocked—at the same time wondering if they all know Tom's wife and are curious why I'm hanging around. Would she be here looking at Groucho if I wasn't? Probably already seen him many times.

I'm on my third beer when Tom strolls over. He's in his jeans and cowboy shirt, running his blond mane back with his fingers.

"Sorry, I got involved in some editing—a training film I'm doing."

"I'm ready to go, okay?" I can't make my voice normal.

He doesn't seem to notice. "Sure. I'll grab my bag. Meet you at the car."

He's gone back into the hangar in a snap, and I say a halfhearted good-bye. Dolly says, "See you in the morning." I know she means it as encouragement—that I should come do my jump no matter what happens with Tom.

I wave at her and Owen and try to look cheery. I'm wondering what kind of shape I'll be in by tomorrow.

We drive in silence for a few minutes. He must know something's up and doesn't want to find out what it is. I don't want to start, either.

"Did you talk to your wife?"

He stares at the road. "I talk to her off and on."

"Tonight. Did you call her?"

He goes to his shirt pocket and pulls out a cigarette.

"Do you smoke in the car?"

"No." He pushes the button to open the window and throws the cigarette out. "Listen. I only want to talk to you. I never want to talk to my wife. Once in a while, I have to."

"From what I heard, it seems like a regular thing."

"It's a financial problem. I've put a lot of money in the house, and she won't make a decent settlement. We've been over and over this."

"She comes here, doesn't she? Everybody at the drop zone knows her."

"She used to jump. Not anymore. People around here don't know anything about what's going on. Look—I told you it's over and that I'm just trying to work things out the best I can. I love you, and I can't treat you right if I'm broke. I want the money that's mine, that's all."

"She skydives?"

"Not anymore." He turns toward me and I can see the glare in those big blues. I don't know if it's passion for me or hate for her. I want to believe it's both.

"She's doesn't love me. It's sadistic. She treats me like shit and calls it love—always has. I thought I could show her how people in love act with each other, but it never worked. It took me three years to realize she's too self-absorbed to learn anything. She doesn't have a clue how to love. She's just a controlling bitch—I'm sorry—and she's got the reins right now."

"What do you mean?" I'm feeling hostile, not accepting this. It's so easy to say.

"It's probably not her fault. She grew up in wealth, big Palm Beach house—right on the beach—maids, whatever she wanted, but her parents were alcoholics. She was constantly being shipped out with her mother whenever there was a fight. His family had all the money."

"I don't want to know about her."

"I'm trying to explain. I knew you wouldn't have anything to do with me if you knew I was still tangled up. I'm guilty, but it's only for a short while longer—now I've found you, and I can't lose you. If I have to give Swan all my money, I will."

"Swan?" My head whirls—Aunt Swan, the one with all the money? The one Bradley said would buy Tom a truck?

I swallow. "Are you having sex with her?"

Tom takes a deep breath and shakes his head. "No, for Christ sake. It's been months. She's seeing somebody else, but she doesn't know I know."

I look into those eyes for truth, but they're so beautiful, I stop searching and let myself drown. How many times am I going to change my mind? I can't bear to lose him. The skydiving and my new life are all tied up with him. I don't want to isolate myself in the loneliness that now will be even more intense. I can feel it all around me in the blackness outside the car, the eternal view of cane fields from my office window, endless to the horizon. Days—and worse, nights—with nothing besides my work. How can I jump out of an airplane in the morning if it's all over between us?

He pulls onto the gravel road to his place and parks next to my car in front of the trailer. I know I should slide right out of his passenger side into the driver's seat of my own, but my ass won't lift. I'm hopeless. I scrunch down to look at the sky ahead. There are a million stars, with no lights to dim them.

Tom comes around and opens my door. All I have to do is take two steps to leave him forever. I can be gone before he knows it, lock the car and look straight ahead so I can't see his face.

"Let's go inside. I want to show you how much I love you." He moves close to me, but not touching, door key held out in his fingers. If I move away, he won't try to stop me.

"Inside?" he asks.

I feel the rough ground under my feet, the cool night on my face, and I smell the slight tang of beer and peppery cigarette a foot from me, his light cologne, him.

My mind empties. I tremble as the wave of paralysis sweeps through me. He sees my slight movement and takes my hand to pull me up. My body feels heavy, but I follow him inside. He drops the keys on the table and grabs me and crushes me to his chest until the ache of knowledge is squeezed out and all I can feel is the intense heat between us.

He picks me up and walks toward the bedroom. I see our reflection in the window as we pass it, my body looking childlike and helpless, my legs dangling from his strong arms, the solid intention on his face. I know he's still involved with his wife, sexually and otherwise, and he's not going to give her up anytime soon. He might give me up if he has to choose. I'm powerless. Surrender is a feeling I should despise.

I WAKE UP SEVERAL TIMES DURING the night and look to see if he's still there. I can't sleep without a toe touching his calf. I dream that she's there, too, and in the morning, I come to consciousness with the hovering feeling of a beautiful slender blonde, soft voice and touch, the remains of a dream. This isn't the vision I want of her, not the one he's given me. It's the incarnation of my worst fear.

He makes love to me slowly, with much kissing, and I don't do anything, just let myself sink under him. He slides into me and my fears are overpowered by sensation. I'm just a human being, after all. I need love. I didn't intend to get involved with a married man. I didn't start it. If it wasn't me, it would be somebody else. I'm comforted by that, and then I let it go. My arms clasp his neck and I grab a handful of his hair in back and wrench up from the bed. Passion turns me into muscle and heat.

When I get out of the shower, he has cinnamon toast and coffee ready. We sit down at the small table.

He touches my chin with his finger and tilts my face upward. "This whole thing's gone on too long. I've got to bring it to a head."

I look straight on and take a bite of my toast. I don't want promises he's incapable of keeping. I don't want lies.

We have to drive separately to the drop zone because I'll need my car later to go home. I've got appointments in the morning, and besides, I haven't been invited. I realize it's convenient for him.

We're not seen arriving in the same car. I can't help thinking along those lines.

Dolly sends me into the hangar, where Gerson is waiting for me. I have to put Swan out of my mind to learn the skills that will keep me alive. It flashes across my mind that I could be suicidal. Some people would think so. But I know I'm not. I don't have to give up Tom.

The morning flies by. Between listening, answering Gerson's trick questions, and taking notes, I'm caught up completely. The main thought in my mind is how well I'll be able to judge my landing, to face into the wind and flare at the right time for a soft step down. As long as I keep my sanity, I should be able to find my way back to the airport, staying far away from the power lines and barbed-wire fences that lie in the wrong direction. "If you hit the power lines," Gerson says with a stone face, "don't touch two at a time." I feel my eyes bug out. He laughs. "You won't."

He walks with me through the hangar and outside toward manifest. I'm reviewing in my head the most important things he's told me: No matter what position I get into, arch and I'll straighten out. Pull at five thousand feet. Don't fly over anything I don't want to land on. Turn into the wind to land. Flare to cut the speed as my feet reach ceiling height.

There's the radio, too. Gerson will be in contact as I fly toward the airport—that is, if the McDonald's down the road doesn't interfere on the frequency. When I need instructions to land, I expect to hear "Big Mac, large fries, and a strawberry shake." I hope I have the mind to remember to flare.

After he manifests us, I walk with Gerson back to the hangar to get geared up. I see skydivers of all ages, sexes, and sizes. A ninety-pound Asian woman stands in a group of five men, their heads to the center, arms locked, dirt diving. They're laughing, obviously not feeling near death. These people all survived many, many times. The odds are that I will, too. I only have to think reasonably.

My hands are shaking as I choose my goggles and helmet, and I wonder what kind of panicked look I have on my face. I pull on the yellow jumpsuit and fumble to zip it up. Gerson helps me put my arms into the straps of the rig, then begins attaching all the buckles and clips. I'm not worried about jumping out of the airplane; it's the landing I fear. There's no way to practice. I still wonder if I'll recognize the airport and if I'll be able to control the canopy enough to land into the wind gently. Work would be tough with a broken leg.

Tom, Gerson, Neil, and I walk out to the plane, approaching the Porter, a taxi yellow bird, from the rear. All the rules and precautions are running through my head, and I'm trying to sort out the most important. I'm afraid of overload, forgetting all of it. Even when my whole life depended on passing a test in vet school, I never felt the physical grip of fear like this, a layer of oil sloshing through my guts, the air squeezed out of my lungs, the feeling of a steel collar around my throat, no saliva in my mouth.

I'm told to put my helmet on as I get into the plane. The words seem to come from far away, somewhere in the real world that I've detached myself from. My normal sensations are dulled beneath the fear. We begin to ascend.

Tom asks me to recite the dive flow. I make my voice steady as I go through the exit, the circle of awareness, the three practice ripcords—arch, look, grab, recover—altitude awareness, the wave-off, the ripcord. Then comes the look, a count of three as the chute opens, the brake release and toggle testing. I'm thinking, Remember not to release the brakes if there are line twists. Think, remember. I've always been good at following instructions. I just need to accept that I could die, be maimed or paralyzed—the general possibilities of life I've always ignored. Then think, act rationally. Let it be.

The sky is dazzling out the window—a color I think of as Tom-eye blue. The ground is so far away that it seems impossible to hit it, fluffy clouds thick enough to hold me up. I try to convince myself of that. I begin to pray, ask help from all the saints in heaven, my deceased grandparents. Gerson points to the altimeter on his wrist and tells me to put on my goggles and helmet. "Ready to skydive?"

"Yes." This is my voice, I realize.

When the door opens, the noise and cold blast of air tear away any remaining sanity. Tom and Gerson crouch an inch from that open gap of wild blue air, spotting the airport for our exit, not even holding on. It's perfectly rational, I tell myself—they're wearing parachutes.

Jason yells, "Cut," and Neil climbs out, until all I can see are his fingers curled around the edge of the open doorway. My thoughts stop when Tom motions me toward the door. The chute on my back feels heavy, my legs stiff. I can barely move, but somehow I drag myself. "Why am I doing this?" I ask aloud, but I can't hear my words. Nobody answers.

Now I'm squatting with my left leg back, my right foot outside the door, on the step. My hands are on my thighs, nothing holding me. Air rushes by. Tom's face is an inch from mine. His eyes are wide, staring. He's waiting for me to start the exit. "Check in," I yell into his face.

"Okay."

I turn to Gerson on my left. "Check out."

"Okay."

I lean out barely—"Ready." In—"Set." Arch—I'm out the door, loose, unstable, unfocused in the blue. I remember to push my hips forward, get my arms square and back, my legs out. I look at the horizon and check my altimeter. Look left. There's Tom, holding me steady. I look right. Gerson is smiling. I wait. He gives the sign.

I check my altimeter: eight thousand feet. Time for practice ripcord pulls. I look at my hip, don't see the neon orange of the handle, but my palm touches it. I reach my other hand above my head and try to keep stable for three pulls. I feel the pressure of the relative wind against my arms as I move them. I feel I'm balancing on a thin wire down my middle.

I check the horizon, altimeter, check left, check right. I finally notice Neil smiling to my front right. I forgot he was filming. Tom and Gerson swing me around. It's exhilarating. I glance down at the altimeter and the needle is just hitting the five thousand mark. I wave off and grab and give it the long pull, straight forward and out. Miraculously, the cord is in my hand. I look over my shoulder, at the same time feeling a lift, my legs flinging upward, the colors unfurling above me. I'm pulled into a vertical position, lungs expanding with pure universe.

I check the canopy, knowing already from the calm that it's doing the job. There's a line twist, but it jerks out by itself. The slider comes down and everything's fine. I reach up and feel the toggle loops and peel them from the Velcro, yank them down in front of me, test left, right, down again. The airport is right there, in front of me. I'm a bird sailing downwind, alone and exhilarated.

It seems a long time in the air until Gerson comes on the radio. He tells me to keep my arms straight up and head for the airport. He talks me into my landing, but the wind is strong and I can't make it to the target. I see where I'm coming down but don't know what to do about it. With all the grass around me, I land on the asphalt runway, feetfirst, gently, then bump down on my ass as the wind catches the chute. I grab the left toggle and pull, as I've been told to, so I don't get dragged and scrape equipment or skin. I'm amazed that my mind hasn't left me.

I yank off the helmet and I'm smiling inside and out as I gather up the yards of fluff and hold them to my body. I begin the trudge back, knowing I've got to do this again, repeat this feeling I've been searching for all my life. Tom is straight ahead, smiling and watching me walk, shining with the glow of the sun across his face and the wind rippling his hair. The world is green grass and blue sky.

Neil is pointing his camera my way, and I can't stop grinning. Amazing happiness. The thought of Tom fucking his wife comes into my head and I don't care. I take a deep breath and inhale the sweetness of orange blossoms, mixed with the stench of sugarcane processing, an odor as powerful as fresh dog shit—it's all a delight, wonderful.

MONDAY MORNING, I DRIVE BACK home in the best of moods—the adrenaline cure, I'll call it. Whatever happens, I've got a skydive and Tom to look forward to on the weekend. It's enough to keep me happy. I realize how my life has changed. Work has lost priority. Maybe it's normal, more well-rounded. But I've always hated normal. Why?

I get out of the car and look up at the sky. Pure blue—it rushes through me, a sensation re-created. It brings back the feeling of Sunday morning, stepping out of Tom's trailer, wondering if I would be able to do my jump. Wanting to jump and being terrified to jump. I pointed to the sky. "Look at all those clouds," I said to Tom. "Look at all the holes," he replied. His voice was expansive with the tone of positive eternal truth. I loved him for it—even though my excuse was blown.

For a Monday morning, I feel so good that I go back inside and beep him. I just want to tell him how much he's added to my life before I have to plow into the heavy workweek. Of course, I can only wait a few minutes, and he doesn't call me back. This is one of his days off, so I imagine he's with Swan.

I feel a cloudy mood threatening, but a lightness still bubbles inside my chest. Life is short, and could be shorter—I'm jumping out of a plane again next weekend. Nothing matters but the present. I slide into the memory of the rush that comes with the opening of the canopy. Alongside that, Tom's relationship with Swan is meaningless. I call up the surge again, intensify the power by visualizing. I recognize the change in me as physical memory takes over. My breathing accelerates and body heat builds. The exhilaration is incredible, the power of fear. I know it's only adrenaline, but it feels spiritual, like there is something beyond the body, something universal I've tapped into. A chill rushes up my spine and I sigh—*airgasm*. I've heard the word out at the DZ. I've found a level I never knew existed. Maybe it isn't for everybody, but I know it's for me.

In the afternoon, I change clothes to head to the park. I step into my shorts. The phone rings and I pick up.

"It's me, Tom." His voice is low.

"What's the matter?"

"Can you come out here later—as soon as possible?"

"Yes. To the trailer? What's wrong?"

"Jeepers. He had a convulsion or something—drooling, shaking, shitting all over. I don't know what's the matter."

"How's he now?"

"Sleeping. He seems better, but it was bad."

I head to the park immediately. There are no emergencies, so I do the scripts and rechecks, and I finish at two by rescheduling the rhino fecals for the next day. It will be a long day, but right now all I want to do is get over to Tom's and check on Jeepers. I start thinking on the drive over there, always a bad thing. I'm disgusted with myself because I'm more eager to see Tom than the animal. It's almost like I'm glad Jeepers got sick so I have an excuse to get back over there. I shake my head involuntarily—what age will this Jeepers be? As much as I try, I can't make myself feel bad or used. I'm simply happy, despite any doubts. I can't deny that I have stronger feelings about seeing Tom than I do concerning the animal's health. I should be ashamed of my part in this, but the gut feeling of regret isn't there.

Tom's Bronco is out front, so I knock on the door. I wait a few seconds, but there's no sound. I head down the path to the cage. As

I round the bend, I see him sitting on a stool, smoking. He's the perfect Marlboro man with one hand on his hip and his leg crossed over at the knee. I stop to look at him longer. He's off in some daydream as the smoke curls slowly from his open lips. He turns and sees me.

"Des," he says. I hear affection in his voice and see his eyes roam over me. He smiles and it grows slowly wider, until it covers his face.

"I finished up early."

As we meet in front of the cage, he takes me in his arms and lifts me off my feet to kiss me.

I slip back down to the ground, as much as I don't want to. "Let me get a look at Jeepers."

He lets me go and opens the cage. I step in. The cat sleeping on its side is neither of the cubs I've seen. I move slowly through the examination, trying not to stare at the obvious splotched markings that Jeepers cannot have developed. I believe I've seen at least three different cubs by now. I'm thinking of what I should say. I get to the temperature, lift the tail.

"Tom." He comes over and holds the feline by the shoulders.

I point. "This is a female."

He nods.

My face is close to his. I smell his clean breath. I'm in a position where I might normally go for a kiss. I stare, but he doesn't blink. "This isn't Jeepers," I say.

His hand comes up and pushes the hair back from my eyes. I soften with the caresses on my temple.

"How is she?" Tom asks.

I remove the thermometer and read it. "Normal."

He watches me, hands on his hips, as I put away my instruments. He's not about to volunteer any information. "I'll send out the blood work just to make sure, but I'm thinking she's had a tonic clonic seizure. She looks healthy otherwise, fed well, wherever she came from. "I reach into my bag to get the syringe. "Hold her again."

I finish the procedure and put the blood sample in my bag. I snap it shut and stand. He still says nothing, looks at me straight on. "Let's go inside," I tell him. "I need to clean up a little."

My mind is a tempest in hell as I walk back to the trailer. He follows me, and I know he can tell by the pace that I'm ready to ask solid questions. I sense him walking sullenly behind me, almost aggressively rejecting what I have to say before he hears it. I'm seething, and defensive, even though I'm the one in the right. I should never have let myself get into a position like this. It violates my belief in myself, and I swore I'd never do that again.

I brush aside a ficus root and concentrate on putting one foot in front of the other into the loose sand. I don't need another haunting memory, another scar on my pride, a new source of doubt.

I scuff the sand off my shoes and open the door. Tom's right behind me, but I go straight to the bathroom. I hear him open the refrigerator—probably needs a beer. Yeah, have a beer and go to hell, arrogant bastard. I hear him lighting up a cigarette and the acrid smell follows. He's smoking more lately, or at least around me. I wash my hands as if I'm preparing for surgery, then splash water on my face. I visualize him on the couch, smoking and swigging beer and maybe looking at the skydive magazine on the coffee table. Nothing will touch him, no matter how angry I get. His answer will be take it or leave it, no matter that he says he loves me.

I dry my face and walk out. He looks up.

I stand in front of him, my arms straight at my sides. "Tell me the truth. Where's Jeepers? Why do you have a female cub in the cage?"

"You really want to know?" His voice is steady, his blue eyes bright.

I stare at him. "No. Absolutely not." I should pick up my purse and head on out, never to return. Like the last time, I get no farther than a twitch. Leave, I tell myself. Go back to the safe, honorable world I've built. But I'm not the woman I should be. My feet will not lift off the rug. The tension goes out of me and I collapse on the couch beside Tom. I put my hand on his thigh.

He puts his arm around my shoulder and cuddles me to him for a kiss. I close my eyes.

"You have to trust me. I'm not doing anything illegal. I want to be damn sure no animals come to harm—that's why I asked for your help."

"So what the fuck's going on?" I barely breathe the words.

"Just a little retail to supplement my income."

"You're buying and selling lion cubs?"

"On a very limited basis. I have some rich friends that like to impress their other rich friends. It all got started by word of mouth. First one was just a favor."

"How many of your friends want lions?"

"You'd be surprised. I guess it's a small network by now in several parts of the country. I don't know all these people—but they're loaded. They're willing to pay a lot of money for me to find them a healthy animal, and I make the arrangements to hand-deliver. They can afford to have the best care possible. Most of these cubs go home to their own private keepers."

"Where do you get the cubs?"

He shifts his body and puts his free arm under my hips to slide me closer to his side. He lifts my legs over his. "I have a deal with one of the guys at Lion Country—he's the one recommended you. He has contacts with small private zoos—I think he does it on the Internet. He orders the cubs for the park and we pick 'em up. A lot of these zoos won't sell to individuals; if they do, they're probably not reputable."

"That should tell you something."

"I swear—these cubs get the best of care. I couldn't live with myself otherwise."

"Do you see them after they're sold?"

"Not usually, but we're talking about cool people here. I've spoken to all of them. They wouldn't buy an animal they couldn't afford to treat right. That's part of the kick—getting the fancy cage and showing all their friends."

I can't stop shaking my head. "I don't like it. What happens to those cubs when they become adults?"

Tom shrugs. "Mostly zoos—same place they would've ended up."

I know he's probably right about that. I feel the hot blood slowly leaving my face, and acceptance creeps into my voice. "I don't know if it's illegal, but it's still wrong. There's lying involved."

He pulls me toward him. I let myself relax, falling sideways onto his lap. He turns my face up toward his and I turn so I'm on my back, staring up into his unearthly eyes. He strokes my neck and ear. "The only lying I worried about was to you. I don't like keeping anything from you. I'm glad it's all out."

I put my hand up and touch his face. I'm shaking. "Will you stop—just for me?"

He looks so hard into my eyes, I can hardly keep from blinking. "I have one cub on the way. After that, if you still want me to stop, I'll do it—even though the money really helps me out. The skydiving doesn't pay a hell of a lot, you know. You have to do it for the love of the sport." He takes a piece of my hair and bends it under my nose like a mustache. "I wouldn't want to connect you with anything you think is wrong."

I can't help but think back to the day we met in the office. He'd told me he was watching the cub for a guy at the bar. It was a pretty detailed lie. Two thousand dollars, money toward a new parachute. "Remember the story you told me—Jeepers chewing up all your furniture?"

"The first cub did—Jeepers. I got him from a guy at the bar, like I told you. That's what got me started."

Now I can't think clearly. I doubt this story, but I can't set the details in order to know for sure.

"I didn't know you then. I never figured we'd be together—in love. It wasn't much of a lie."

I want to drop it. If I refuse to help, he'll keep selling cubs without vet care. "Okay," I say, "just one more. Maybe I can talk to the adoptive parents and make sure they're prepared with what's needed."

"Yep. No problem. You can make sure everything's perfect. You'll see what I mean."

chapter

FIFTEEN

AS IT GETS CLOSER TO THE WEEK-
end, the problems with Tom dim in importance. Recalling the
shriek of the engine and roar of the wind outside that door clears
my thoughts. I tell myself half-seriously, If I die on level two, I
won't have to deal with Tom and the heartache.

Saturday afternoon, I notice myself humming as I get into the
car to start my drive to the drop zone. My energy is high, even
though I've had a full morning, and not much sleep the night
before, since Tom made a late visit. I ask myself why I'm going to
jump, and I truly don't know, but it doesn't matter. The need is
beyond a short-lived adrenaline rush. The fear is so painful that the
rush can't equal, much less surpass, it. I believe that somehow the
essence of myself, some part too deep and irrational to explain, is
fulfilled by skydiving. Forcing myself to look death in the face puts
me in a rare position to gain self-knowledge. I've noticed how
unusually nice and considerate skydivers are, and I think it's
because they're always prepared to die. When life is perceived as
short, pettiness is useless and unnecessary. Everybody is connected
in spirit.

I pass two crackling-hot burns in the cane fields on my way to
the DZ. One is near the road, and as I clear the smoke, I barely miss
a rabbit on fire, panicked, streaking to beat its death, unknowlingly
feeding the flames on its body with the air, heading straight into
traffic. The sight makes me sad, helpless—nothing I can do. There
are dead snakes, rats, and other rabbits on the road. I start to sink

into depression, but the excitement ahead picks me back up. I think of Tom and that open door into the blue, and I'm saved from pondering the pitiful details of life.

I get to the DZ and walk across the grass to the manifest building. Everybody I pass greets me. "What level today?" a redheaded guy asks. I tell him two, and he gives me a thumbs-up. Everybody seems to know I'm in training. I pass a group of eight doing a dirt dive. Someday I'll join them, when I'm good enough. Jump out of a plane and gain a family, a life. Why hadn't I thought of it long ago?

I see Tom's car parked on the side of the hangar, but he's not in sight. I walk into the manifest building. Dolly and Aimee are there behind the counter.

The reality triggers a wave of fear that presses me hard into the floor. I wave as I walk toward them, trying to be normal, not look as if I'm in line to be the next human sacrifice. "I'm ready for level two," I tell them, pushing for enthusiasm through a tight throat. I feel like I've just set down a heavy load, used all my energy to get the sounds across the space between us. I feel pale and cold, like a statue. I wonder if everybody feels this way when they come to this point—given a terrifying choice, nothing concrete to gain, your life as the stakes, and you must take the challenge. I remind myself of the physical exhilaration and centered mind I had minutes before—gone. Gone with the wind.

Dolly calls for Gerson because Tom's up with a tandem. She tells me I'll have a short briefing and practice; then the two of them will take me up for level two.

Gerson goes to manifest us, and I wait in the hangar, studying the aerial view of the airport. At least I'll recognize it now, and unless something crazy happens with the wind, I won't have any problem making it back. I go over and over the pattern for landing in the student field. All the cautions are running through my head. Malfunctions flood my brain—which ones to cut away, which ones to correct.

I feel someone looking over my shoulder.

"What level you on?"

I turn to a tall, dark man. "Two—any minute now."

"Nervous?"

"Can you tell?" I try to give him a normal smile.

He laughs. "You're supposed to be."

I shrug. His eyes have sparks. He's enjoying my fear, as if it's just silliness.

"You live around here?" he asks.

"Pahokee."

"Yeah? I'm in Palm Beach." He puts out his hand and takes mine. "My name is Roth." He squeezes my hand softly. "You're beautiful—nervous or not."

"Destiny—Desi for short."

"Beautiful." He smiles. "Will you be my destiny?"

"I've heard that one—a lot."

"What load you on?"

Over Roth's shoulder, I see Tom walking up to us. Before I can say a word, he steps in front of Roth and puts a hand on each of my shoulders. "We're on the next load. Ten minutes to be out on the grass," he says. "Pick a helmet and goggles."

"I didn't even hear the twenty minute announcement yet."

"Too busy talking." He looks at Roth. "Haven't seen you around for a while. Been traveling the world, I guess."

"Yeah. Traveling, grabbing some sky here and there. Just back to check a few things."

"Goin' up?"

"Sure."

"What load?"

"Eight."

"Care to try that heads-down dive again, the one we fucked up on last year?"

"You fucked up on." Roth turns to me and winks.

Tom laughs.

He sounds odd. I'm not sure whether they're kidding around or what. I open my mouth to say bye to Roth, but Tom grabs me by the arm and turns me, so I'm yelling it over my shoulder. He leads me to the rack of rigs and lifts one onto my back. "Roth's a smart-ass—a skygod in his own mind. Remember to listen to your instructors and ignore what anybody else tells you."

"He wasn't telling me anything about skydiving."

Tom nods his head. "Well, he's an ass, whatever he was telling you."

He slips the rig over my shoulders. I wonder if Tom is jealous. That would be refreshing, but probably they're just rivals. I stop thinking about him and Roth and anything besides throwing myself out of that plane.

My stomach is cramping all the way up, and I have to concentrate to breathe normally. Finally, we reach altitude. Gerson motions and I make my way to the door.

We set up and I turn to Gerson, go through the routine, then turn to Tom.

He gives me a big smile and I wait. "Okay."

I arch out as Tom and Gerson hold on. There's a fast flash of being out of control and then I'm stable, reaching terminal velocity, the roar of wind the only reminder that I'm falling at tremendous speed. Now there's Neil in front of me somehow, filming, like before. I do my turns. Check altitude. I know I've done well. At five thousand feet, I wave off and pull. There's a slight delay when the pilot chute gets caught in the burble—dead air above my back—but I twist slightly and look up, as I've been told to do, and the small chute flies, pulling out a billow of bright orange. I feel it, the swing to a vertical position, and I grab the risers and watch the nylon unfurl into the rectangle, a sight that amazes me once again.

I expect immediate calm, but it doesn't come. I'm in the mist of a cloud, rocking left and right. I study the canopy—vent folds. I peel the toggles from the Velcro and give a strong pull on both. The edges of the canopy straighten right out. I'm proud of myself, a burble and a low-speed malfunction corrected. Ordinary stuff, for sure, but a new experience for me. I test the steering lines, left and right. Everything works.

I look for the airport. Below, a film of white is all I can see. What next? I feel my heart beating. I've used some time making adjustments, and I'm worried I won't make it back. I check altitude—3,500 feet, plenty, unless I'm headed in the wrong direction. I remember I've been told to circle if I can't see the airport, but what if I'm far away? I start making a slow circle right. I wish I would hear from Gerson on the radio.

It's a few long seconds till I pass through the haze—time has new meaning for me now—and there it is, the clean layout of runways directly in front of me. I turn a little left to cut a diagonal to the holding area over the cane fields until I reach one thousand feet, when I'll move into my landing pattern. I take my time doing some S-turns and hanging out into the wind, feeling good. Lake Okeechobee flattens the distance, blue, everywhere blue.

As the altimeter passes the thousand mark, I turn myself downwind and glide. The radio sputters, "If you can hear me"—crackle, crackle—"if you can hear me"—crackle, crackle. It must be Gerson saying to do something. As I sink to five hundred feet, I'm over the student landing field and his voice finally comes in clear. He tells me I'm doing well. I start my downwind run, and he cues me when to turn crosswind, then into the wind. Two hundred feet below me, the ground rolls like a giant spool of grass carpet, sliding wide and fast as I get closer and closer. At ceiling height, I flare, feel the pause, and touch down feetfirst, then plop on my butt, ungraceful, but soft. I'm ecstatic. I'm amazed. Who would think falling on my ass in a field would make me happy? I look up at all the holes. This isn't so crazy. I'm Mom's daughter, after all.

Neil comes walking up, filming, as I begin to loop up the yards of line and pile them on top of the canopy. I know I'm not doing it right, but I'll catch the technique on another lesson. I feel a grin on my face big enough for a clown. I try not to look at the camera, not to show my intense relief, but he comes around and I grin upward. "Alive again," I tell him.

He shifts the camera downward and I know he's finished filming. I unclip my helmet and pull it off. My hair falls in a mass over my face and Neil laughs as he walks away. I throw back my head and laugh more loudly than I expect.

I set the helmet on the ground with the ripcord so I can have two hands free. I press the toggles into the Velcro, then start bundling the pile of nylon, bringing it up from the bottom, as I've been shown, until it's a fairly tight wad with the pilot chute on top. I pick everything up and start walking, feeling out of breath and loving it.

Tom is nowhere in sight. Gerson is waiting for me near the runway and he gives a thumbs-up and walks beside me back to the hangar. "I have a training and a jump. I'll debrief you after that," he says.

"Fine," I say. He seems solemn, but I know I passed.

I find a spot in the hangar and drop my canopy. Tom must have had a jump right after, because he's still nowhere around. He should be a magician. I head over to DZ Mom's trailer to get a soda. She invites me to come inside. I go around back, pull the door open, and sit on a stool next to the stainless-steel work area facing the landing field. I feel more relaxed than I ever have in my whole life.

Mom hands me a diet Pepsi and starts telling me about her many past jobs, including floral arrangement and day care, leading up to how she happens to be cooking at the drop zone. I can tell she knows everything that goes on. She doesn't skydive herself, but her husband, Jacques, does, and she enjoys feeding the skydivers and talking.

I hear the sound of canopies in flight and look for the next load to land. Someone comes in to the far left of the student field and lands feetfirst, then collapses onto his knees and down onto his face. "Ooh, that looks like it hurt," I say.

Mom squints. "Who's that?" she asks.

I shrug.

"He's not getting up. He's unconscious. Look." She yells to her husband and I hear the door of their camper open. "Jacques, see what's the matter."

He steps out to where we can see him. "That's Roth, I think. Yeah, it's Roth!" Jacques takes off running, and three guys come tearing out of manifest.

I stand and look. The guy moves onto his hands and knees, but he's not trying to get up, might be holding his head.

I recognize Tom's canopy and watch him swoop and tiptoe down close by. I realize this would be load eight, so he must have gotten on with Roth. He pulls off his helmet. I'm thinking I don't remember Tom wearing a helmet before—maybe he only wears it when he's doing something tricky.

Mom and I go out and stand in front of the kitchen to watch. Tom drops his container on the ground and goes to Roth just as the others are getting there. Everyone's crowding around. The last jumpers are landing farther down the field. I hear yelling. Tom walks back to his rig and picks it up. He walks away, heading toward the hangar. Two guys help Roth to his feet. As they walk closer, blood is visible halfway down the front of his white jumpsuit. They turn and go into manifest. Jacques comes walking back toward the trailer.

"Oh shit. They must have hit in freefall," Mom says to me. "The two of them are too cocky for their own good. That could have been a disaster."

I've already been thinking about that, thinking that Roth must have had a Cypres computer that fired his reserve, or he would be dead night now.

Jacques stands and turns as he talks to us, watching as the last person lands in the student field. "They were free flying, transitioning from a stand-up to a head-down face-to-face, each doing the opposite move. During the switch, Tom's knee connected with Roth's jaw."

"Ooh. How would that happen?" I ask him.

"Tom says Roth hit into him, and Roth says it was the other way round—hard to know without video. That shit happens fast." Jacques shakes his head. "They're taking Roth to the hospital— broken jaw, it looks like."

Mom looks at me and shakes her head. "Those two have been at it for a long time—even before they were in-laws. You'd think they'd fucking know better." She turns and goes back to the kitchen.

Her words land in my lap, even though I'm standing up. Roth must be Swan's brother. And what did she mean—they've been at skydiving or at each other for years? Surely the rivalry wasn't strong enough for Tom to bash Roth in the mouth purposely in free fall. I wonder whether Tom knew that Roth had a Cypres. Of course, that's a moot point—ridiculous to think of—purposely knocking somebody unconscious in free fall would be as good as murder.

I find Tom in the hangar. I need to tell him bye. I have to go home and catch up on paperwork and laundry. I ask about Roth. Tom doesn't seem to want to talk about the details. "Things happen now and then," he tells me.

I'm not too happy thinking about that on the way home. It's another little panic button I'll be able to press when I'm waiting to take my leap and the epinephrine is flowing through my brain, conjuring up all sorts of reasons not to jump. Get a grip, I tell myself. I'm not going to be doing anything crazy. Nevertheless, I can't get it off my mind all the way home. I can't help but think that Tom and Roth have some problem between them. It bothers me, but I'm afraid to mention it, don't know how to ask for details he'd obviously rather not give.

I don't have a real conversation with Tom until a few days later. He brings up the accident on the phone. "I pulled his ripcord for him," he tells me. "He had the nerve to complain that I was responsible for his jaw, even after I saved his life."

"He didn't have a Cypres?"

"Yeah, he did. But I was there. You can't count on anything but yourself."

"Whew," I say. "I wonder if I'd be able to do that for somebody."

"You won't be flying with anybody but me for a while."

He changes the subject, inviting me over for dinner, and I let the accident drop, but a question keeps coming back to me: If Tom pulled for Roth, wouldn't Tom have landed first because he pulled lower? I don't have enough knowledge to figure it out for sure. Maybe parachute size made the difference, and the directions each flew. I'll have to wait to hear more about it when Roth comes back around.

chapter

SIXTEEN

OVER THE NEXT FEW WEEKS, TOM and I evolve a system where I do a level or two of training on Saturday afternoon, depending on the weather and my work schedule, and he hides out in his cubbyhole in the hangar during the early evening. He's calling Swan, I suppose, while I socialize and drink beer at the fire. Then we head to his place. I make a point not to ask questions—not about Swan or even Bradley, nothing involving family matters. I don't look around where I might find something, even though I leave his place after he does on Sunday morning to drive back to my apartment. He's easy with that, so either there's nothing to be found or he can read me and feels safe.

The skydiving takes up most of my thinking time, so it's easy not to obsess. I roll through the dive flow of the week in my mind whenever I start to think of Tom with Swan. The obvious possibility of death overpowers the threat of their relationship. By the sixth weekend, I'm ready to complete levels seven and eight, the last two. I don't know what I'll do when I'm finished. The idea of buying my own parachute seems crazy, yet I can't afford to keep renting. I can't give it up, either. My whole life has changed.

On levels seven and eight, I'm considered capable of diving out of the plane alone, even though I haven't managed to control my turns yet. Gerson has told me I have to learn to hold a heading to complete the basic skills. Tom has stepped aside, since only one instructor is required on the later levels. He says I can listen better to somebody I'm not involved with. He might be too easy on me.

Whatever. I'm comfortable with Gerson—as comfortable as you can be plummeting at 120 mph.

There's ten minutes to wait for the load, and Gerson has given me a gear check and gone to put on his own rig. Tom comes out of his little office area in the hangar. He looks around to make sure we're alone. "I just had a call from Swan," he says.

"Oh?"

He's scuffing his Tevas, right then left, his jumping sandals, uniform for the experienced jumpers.

"Why are you telling me this?" I ask him. I'm building up anger and impatience. I have a forward and backward roll, controlled turns, tracking, pulling stable, and landing, before I have to think about the rest of my life—or his. "This isn't a good time to talk about it."

"She knows about us and she's threatening to kill you."

"Kill me?" I reach for Tom's arm. "How? She doesn't even know who I am. Does she?"

He takes my hand and squeezes it. "Apparently. She had me followed to your office."

Fear clutches at my guts, but I yank myself out of it. "This doesn't make sense. You said she hated you—you hadn't been together for months. She was just trying to cause you financial trouble." I feel my throat tighten. I've been standing there in thirty pounds of gear feeling fine, ready to jump out of a plane, and now I'm pressed into the concrete floor by the weight of this.

"I know. Now she says we'd be back together if it wasn't for you."

Gerson walks up. "Let's go. You okay?"

I try to shake off my anger. My guts are broiling that Tom would say this now. I know he has never told me the truth where Swan is concerned.

"Sorry. I don't mean to foul up your jump—you'll do fine."

I glare at him. I can't say anything.

Gerson frowns. "You want to cancel? We can always do this tomorrow."

I suck in a breath through my nose. "No. . . . Not a chance. I can't wait to jump out of that plane."

I turn to Tom. I'm shaking, but the words come out loud and clear. "Fuck you. I don't need this shit."

Gerson's eyes widen slightly and he gives Tom a raised eyebrow. I walk past them and don't stop till I'm on the edge of the grass, waiting for the Porter. I'm going to complete my dive flow and finish AFF today, no matter what. Hell, I'll deal with the grief later. Right now, I just want to do my maneuvers and live.

We have a few minutes to wait and Gerson points to a dark cloud in the west. "Good thing we're on this load. We'll beat that rain."

I look at it moving our way. I'm not so sure we'll beat it. "What happens if the parachute gets wet?"

"It's not that. It's painful. In free all, you're coming down faster than the drops, so you're speeding into the pointy sides—so they say. Feels like a million pins. You get red spots all over your neck—on any exposed parts."

I look at the cloud again. "This might not be my day."

"You're tough. You can handle it." He pats my shoulder.

I manage a tight smile.

On the way up, Gerson tells me I can dive right out of the plane into a front somersault to get it out of the way. It seems a good idea since fifty-five seconds is a short space to do all the requirements, especially if I get unstable and have to waste time getting back into the box position. I check my handles and wind my hair up to pin it under my helmet, and I think of Swan. My stomach is a caved-in hollow where the filling presence of Tom has been torn out, but when the door opens to the roar of engine and sky, my mind goes blank and my body moves toward space.

Gerson looks at me and I nod and fall out, headfirst into the unknown. I tumble in some ungraceful position of bent arms and legs, then swing stable as I arch. From there on, I do everything fine. The thrill runs through me as the chute unfurls and I'm snatched by the firm hold of the harness. I'm under control, queen of the sky; I don't care what hell is on earth. The rain has missed us.

My last jump is the hop and pop, and again I put Tom aside and finish what I have to do. It's the long years of stress and study, I'm sure, that help me to conquer the pressure. I slide in on my butt softly.

Gerson is waiting for me outside at the picnic table, and he asks me how the jump went and writes "passed" and "good job" in my logbook. From the door of the plane, he watched me get stable and pull. "You're finished with AFF," he says. "Now you're safe enough to learn how to skydive."

I laugh and nod. I've already had the realization that I'm only beginning to learn control.

"After a few more jumps on your own, we'll transition you to the throw-out pilot chute. You can start doing some two-ways."

I notice he's taking it for granted that I'm going to continue, and that feels right.

I walk through the hangar and everybody asks me how I did or congratulates me. I don't know some of their names—Cindy and Owen are there and Lester and Lee, packing. They're all happy for me. Another crazy joins the ranks.

I get to my car without seeing Tom. He's probably in talking to Swan and still expecting me to spend the night at the trailer with him. It will be good for him to see the empty parking space when he comes out. Then it dawns on me. I'm not ending anything between us. I'm playing some kind of game to make him sorry. Like, if he sees my car gone, he'll give up Swan for me? That's not even the point. He's lied to me. Now she's threatened to kill me. I get in the car and start it up. I don't want him to know I'm devastated.

I don't hear from him on Sunday. I think about him all day,

wondering about the truth of their relationship. Wondering if Swan is really serious. Should I be talking to the police? They'd laugh. My boyfriend's wife, Swan, is threatening to kill me. Doesn't sound like a sympathetic case. Doesn't even sound real. I think about swans, the graceful silhouettes, the pure white feathers, floating puffs on blue water, like clouds. That's the kind of woman for him, not short, top-heavy me.

Yet swans are aggressive. I remember a time from my childhood when I was trying to pet the swans at a lake. I was following one on the bank and it turned its long neck and bit me. It didn't break the skin, but I was so shocked by the sudden change from that soft, pure creature that I cried for a long time. I wonder if Swan's reading things into my name, too. It gives me the creeps. I imagine her words: Going to fuck up Destiny. Destiny's days are numbered. It's like a movie, haunting, but not quite real.

Her voice replays all night in my head, and I alternate from wild anger at Tom to anger at myself for letting it happen, and then into the gut-twisting torture of knowing that I've finished my AFF just in time never to go back there, never to see him again. But that's not a consideration.

IT'S A GRIM MONDAY MORNING, THE
sky outside glaring bright in contrast to my mood. Smoke is in the
air and my throat feels scratchy—a nearby burn, no doubt, blowing my way. I'm too upset to pay the usual attention to the dogs,
and they know it. They've got that hunch to their shoulders, like
they think it's their fault, and I try to pet them and talk perky, but
they know me. By this time, I'm thinking that Tom made up the
whole thing to dump me and keep me away. By noon, my guts and
throat are so tight, I can barely speak. I hoped Tom would call by
then and rationalize the whole thing, say that she threatens things
all the time, and that I shouldn't pay any attention. In my wildest
fantasies, I imagine him saying he'll divorce her now, money problems or not, and end all this sneaking around. I need a few conces-
sions from him.

By that night, I still don't get a call, and Tuesday morning I
can't stand it any longer. I beep him. He calls me back a few minutes later, his voice low and serious. "I'm afraid I'll put you in danger just talking to you."

"So you weren't ever going to call?"

"I was deciding what to do."

"You can't be serious. How would she kill me?"

"She has the money and the mind to do it—people who work
for her. Believe me, she's been controlling me for years."

"It seems to me you have amazing freedom for a married
man."

"It's too much to explain like this. I want to see you."

"Shouldn't I report her threats to the police?"

"No. No good. I need to talk to you first."

I pause. He's not frightening me. "I have a full day, but you could stop in for a few minutes between appointments."

He's silent. For a second, I feel panic rising in my chest at the thought that I'm not going to see him. "No good. I want her to think it's over. She might have somebody watching."

"How could she kill me, then, with some PI knowing all about it?"

"You don't get it. She knows people who'll do anything for enough money. It wouldn't be the first time for murder in their family."

"She has that much money?"

"Yep."

I hear the door to the waiting room open, and cold panic grips my throat. I'm struck with how vulnerable I am here alone. I look at the clock. Okay, it's the next appointment. This time the dachshund needing his shots, tomorrow maybe some cold-blooded slime with a shotgun.

"I can put some things off at the park till tomorrow and make it to your place around five."

"No, you can't come here, either, especially during the day. Meet me at the DZ around nine-thirty. Nobody will be there that late during the week, and I have a key to the gate."

I picture the diamond-shaped road leading to the DZ in both directions, and how black that road is. "The DZ is the perfect place for her to kill me. You know? If she's got somebody following me. You can meet me on the drive to your place."

"There's too much lonely road on the way there. All they'd have to do is run you off the road in the sugarcane. You'd be easy game."

I cringe. "Game?"

"Sorry. That's the way those guys think. It's better if you leave from the park and drive to the DZ. I'd come get you if I could, but that would be the worst—for us to be seen together right now."

"I don't know."

"Des, listen, you have to come. You can easily tell if somebody's following you from the park. If you see a suspicious car, beep me from the first gas station and stay inside till they're gone. Or call the police if you need to. I'll know the meeting's off. Otherwise, the gate at the DZ will be fake locked. Pull in and lock it behind you. I'll be waiting for you in the hangar."

"Unless they force me off the road into the canal on the way in—"

"She wouldn't try anything you might survive—besides, they won't know you're going out there."

"That's a wonderful fucking thought."

"Just meet me there. Don't worry. I know her and her guys."

By evening, I'm nervous yet excited, barely able to eat dinner, even though I forgot to eat all day. I should be strangling in anxiety, but it's the best I've felt since Sunday. The situation isn't real, more like a movie. I'm going to see Tom and get some answers. I feel so good, in fact, it makes me wonder if our relationship is pathological. Here I am, high off the fact that my lover's wife wants to kill me, and we are having a rendezvous to figure out what to do.

As I drive from the park, I go slowly and watch the rearview mirror all the way. People pass, and once I get outside Clewiston, there isn't a light behind me. I take the right leg of the diamond and pull up to the gate. It looks locked, but sure enough, when I check it, the lock falls away. It clanks against the silence, chills me. I look around, feeling like a criminal as I stoop to pick up the lock. I drive through and secure the gate behind me. I know Tom must be waiting in the hangar, so I pull around to the other side. The door is open. Tom steps out of the darkness and into the path of my headlights, with Bear beside him. He motions me to pull inside. I step out of the car.

"Don't want to take a chance of anybody seeing vehicles."

I nod. I look at him straight on. "I don't know what I'm doing here, after all the lies you've told me."

"I'm sorry." His arms go around my shoulders and he presses a firm kiss on my mouth. He runs it down my throat, pulling my hair back and holding my head tight. I feel the answer to the question as a hard need rushes over me. Tom pulls back and the air between us feels cold. "Come on," he says. "Let's take a walk down the taxi-way. It's beautiful at night."

He's out the door, and I'm having to walk fast to keep up. When we get across the parking lot to the runway, he turns and takes my hand.

"Sweetheart, let's just be quiet for a few minutes and enjoy ourselves. We can do that."

I turn and walk with him. There's nothing but blackness in front of me, and the rows of blue and yellow lights a few feet off the ground, stars above us. The sweet peppery smell of orange blossoms hangs in the still, humid air and the sensations sweep me along. We walk farther and I feel myself falling into a romantic trance again.

I stop. "Tom, you told me this is serious. Now give me the facts, so I can make my own judgment."

He wraps his arms around me and buries his face in my hair. He's holding me tight and I can feel his body tense to the point of shaking. "The truth is that I'm married to a cold, controlling woman, who gets her kicks from using me. I need her because I can't afford to skydive for a living if I divorce her. We don't enjoy each other's company. We haven't had sex in more than a year." He stops and strokes my hair, my ear, my neck. "Lately, she's been hanging out with her psychologist—fucking her, I bet—and the only reason she's had me around is to take to her fancy social functions so she can act like the wholesome daddy's girl, with the perfect marriage. The setup doesn't work anymore."

I take his hands from my around me and step back. "So why is she after me?"

"I'm not sure. Either she's afraid somebody in her group of friends will find out about us or she just doesn't want me to be happy."

"Doesn't seem a good enough reason to kill me."

"It's probably jealousy, too, and competition. She can't believe that I would stop jumping through her hoops like a circus animal and get interested in somebody else. She doesn't like to lose. Her ego can't take shit."

I look at him and try to sort it out. My instinct is not to believe a word.

He bends forward and kisses me, a long one that moves around on my lips and gets me wet between the thighs. I can't pull back even now. I'm a much bigger fool than I ever expected to be.

When he stops, I sigh. "Shouldn't we call the police and get her threats on record at least?"

"No. She'll turn that right around against me."

"Tom," I say, staring hard, "we're talking about my life. If we report it, she'll be afraid to do anything."

"I doubt that."

"Why?"

"I have to tell you something else."

I feel my stomach fall. "Okay. What?"

"That lion business—I have to watch it."

"Oh no."

He scuffs the tarmac, looking down in his sorry little-boy style. "Some of those cubs were stolen."

"Fuck. Christ. I knew it. What's the matter with you?" I grit my teeth and cross my arms, as if I can fend off the knowledge. I look at him. "What's the matter with me?"

"I'm not going to keep explaining myself to you. Okay, it's illegal, but those cubs are in better condition than they would have been left where they were. You'll just have to trust me on this."

I start walking fast ahead of him, and it's instant déjà vu. How many times am I going to torture myself, thinking I can give him up? I'm in on it. I've examined three of those cubs. To claim ignorance at this point would be ridiculous. Insanity is my choice. I turn around. Tom's arms are open in front of me.

His head dips instantly over mine, almost like we've rehearsed. He moves me backward onto the grass and I lower myself in front of him. We're both on our knees and he takes my face in his hands and kisses me like I'm the sweetest thing on earth. I don't care what he's done, and I can only hope down to the center of my being that we don't get caught, that my whole life's work won't disintegrate in front of me in a rippling crackle, like acres of cane fields, flames rolling over them too fast even for the rabbits, leaving bones and blackened ground.

His hand moves under my shirt and I whip it over my head, the white T-shirt of surrender. He slips off my shorts and I kick off my shoes as I watch while he unbuttons those jeans. In the blue taxiway lights, I've never seen such a sight. The whole night is the color of his eyes, although I can't see them.

I feel the wet grass under my back and then forget it as he opens me up with his fingers and slides in. It's the second most exciting thing I've ever done on the airfield, and it lasts a lot longer than a skydive.

We get up and I find my T-shirt on the ground and my pants underfoot. We get into our clothes and sit to pull on our shoes.

"Who the fuck's that?" Tom says.

I look up and see lights outside the gate. A car is stopped. It's too far away to see what kind.

"It's her or one of her chumps," Tom says.

"How would she know we were here?"

"I told you—she pays people to keep an eye on us, PIs."

"They can't see us out here. Can they?"

Tom looks around into the darkness. "No. No way. They can't get in, either—not without breaking the lock off."

We sit still and watch. A minute passes and the car idles, the headlights looking dim in the night mist. "Aren't they afraid somebody will see them and call the police?"

"If it's somebody who's been around here, they'll know that Kenny—the watchman—is gone for a couple nights and Bear's in the hangar, just like I did."

The car backs up enough to turn around and it crunches gravel and picks up speed around the left side of the diamond.

"Do you think they were waiting for someone?"

"No idea. Could anybody've seen you pull off the highway?"

"There was nobody behind me. If they were parked with the lights off, I didn't know it."

"See, that's the problem. She knows everything you do, and you have no idea. Unless you move your house, change your job, and stop coming here, she'll always know where to find you."

"Maybe she's just trying to scare me." I look into his eyes. "You're scaring me."

"I'm being realistic. I know her family, and they don't have a problem doing whatever's necessary."

I get that feeling again of being in a movie. A chill lodges between my shoulders. "I sure don't feel like driving home."

"Let's go to my place. They've already made their move for the night."

"Sure?"

He nods, looks at me hard.

I'm not so sure of that, but he pulls me to him for another kiss and I let my body take over. I'm in it, hell or high water now, stolen animals and all. Who knows what else? I can't fool even myself any longer.

When we get out of the cars at the trailer, Tom wraps his arm around me and nearly drags me inside, he's moving so fast. He tells me to get my clothes off while he hides my car.

He's back in two minutes and up against my body, his mouth hot over mine. I feel his hard cock pressing into my hip and I realize he's already charged up again with the excitement of this insanity. *Accomplice* comes into my head. Tom pulls off my shorts and I watch his head between my thighs. I start to feel the meaning of the word *accomplice* as it vibrates into my brain—*accomplice, comply, complicity.* Prickly words to swallow. Tom's face is moving up and down, like he's nodding and nodding again. Yes, yes. His tongue is hot. Everything is fading. Keep it going . . . keep it going. I deserve him—and love—before I die or have to kill myself.

LATER THAT NIGHT, WE LIE CURLED together in Tom's bed, talking for a long time. He tells me how he and his mom moved around a lot. He never knew his father. It's the first time he's ever opened up about his past. He admits to serving some short periods in jail before he was married, coming close to big trouble when he got into a cycle of cocaine use. He made a turnaround when he met Swan, but his obsession with her replaced one addiction with a worse one.

I'm jealous hearing about her, but I know it's not rational, and I keep quiet and stroke Tom's chest. I can't ask him to change the past.

He says she was different then, or at least he thought so. Maybe she just enjoyed being worshiped, until she wore it out—like everything else in her life.

He's more tender than usual, and I'm nearly calm, until he reminds me once more of her threats. "I'll protect you," he says, and puts his arm across my ribs. It's only seconds until I hear his light snoring.

I lie awake for hours, thinking about the rich girl and wondering how much power she has. It's hard for me to think of a civilized woman hiring a hit man, but Tom seems convinced. There are so many places I'm alone each day. I could be killed and my body dumped with the gators—or thrown out on the veldt with the lions. I'm not sure they would eat all the evidence, but Swan would probably think so. My office is another easy setup. There's a good distance between my place and both neighbors, purposely set up for when dogs are being kept overnight for treatment. Nobody would pay any attention if they did hear a racket.

I don't fall asleep until dawn. When I wake up again, the clock says 7:30. I hear Tom in the bathroom and realize I need to get up and fly if I'm going to shower and make it home in time for an 8:30 appointment. It's just a dog for a rabies shot, and I don't have anything else until noon. I think for a second that maybe I have the woman's number in my car and I could call and cancel. The next thing I know, I'm waking up to a clock that says 9:30. No sound of Tom. He must have left. I'm struck with a burning flash of guilt. That's one patient gone—more if she spreads the word. It's a clear sign that my life is beginning to come apart. Yet, I've never lived so free of loneliness—with a love of life I never knew existed, despite the threats. I just have to keep my discipline.

On Thursday, Tom calls to make sure everything's okay, and he warns me over and over not to leave the doors unlocked or go out alone at night. I get a shiver now and then, but his extra attention almost makes up for it. I know I'm being a fool, and I don't care. He tells me that he's not even speaking to Swan anymore, and he's ready to divorce her, no matter about the money. He says he just has to lay low at his trailer for a while, not draw attention to us until the divorce papers are signed.

Friday, I wake up exuberant. There's no explanation for it, other than a change in brain chemistry. I'm full of energy and ready to catch up on the backlog of fecals and vaccinations I've been letting pile up at the park. I get to the park around two and check my notes. Besides the fecals and vaccinations, there are three notes from keepers about animals that need checking. It will take me till dark, if I dare stay to finish up.

I hear Nibblefoot scrounging around in her cage. I walk over. Her water is nearly empty and her pellets are gone. I feel guilty again. I'm ashamed of myself for letting things go with the ani-

mals because of the situation I've gotten myself into. I fill Nibble's
bottle and dump in some food. She sniffs my finger and I reach in
and pull her out. She sits in my hands, and I give her a kiss on her
pink ears. "Hey, girl," I say. She was my only friend before Angel
and Clue. For a second, I get the memory of how I used to feel
when I started my job at the park—proud and free—refreshed with
the idea that I had gotten what I always wanted with my own hard
work and ability, a self-made woman, and nobody could diminish
that. Now it's possible that I've thrown it away for a man, an obsession. If I have to call in the police to save my life, I risk a connection
with Tom and his animal theft that will ruin my reputation. I'll lose
my job, and possibly go to prison. Everything gone down the tube
because of a fatal lack of judgment.

I put Nibblefoot back in her cage and start working as fast as I
can, preparing the slides and searching for ascarids, trying to concentrate on what's important at the moment. Already, skydiving
has taught me perspective.

It's seven o'clock when I look up from the microscope. I realize
I'd better get out to see the sick animals and shoot some with
dewormer before there's a shift change and the keepers leave. I lock
the door and go out to my little zebra truck. I'm struck by the paint
job shining in the sunset. It reminds me again—I'm where I always
wanted to be.

I drive out to section five to see about Saba, a giraffe that was
reported as having a limp. When I get into that section, I pull off
the road and drive through the field, looking for him. I finally think
I see him beyond a group of trees, eating leaves. There's not
enough room for me to drive the truck between the trees and the
fence, and although I know better than to go on foot, I don't want
to wait for him to finish his nibbling and come out to meet me.
Could be dark.

I park on the side of the road and hike between the bushes so I
can come up behind him and get a look. I've seen a giraffe take

down a metal structure with three men on it, while they were trying to treat him, so I don't want to get anywhere he might be able to reach me. I figure I'll keep a tree in between him and me and see what I can. As I come up close, I see that it is Saba, and he's really ripping away at something, like he's starved. I saw his regular feed on the way in, and normally giraffes like that better than stripping the trees, so it's weird behavior for him to be back here by himself. An animal alone often means illness. In this case, I look at his legs to see if he's got an abrasion that might have become infected.

I can't see from this angle, so I move out from the tree a little to get a better look. I glance up to see if he's aware of me, and I notice that he's not eating leaves off the tree, but something that's been stuffed between the branches. It's not a vine or anything that could grow there, more like a small bale of something that's been placed.

The hair rises up on my neck, like an animal's fear response, something that I don't remember ever feeling in my life, a paralyzing prickle. I'm thinking that this has something to do with me. I glance behind me, but there's nothing. The thick bushes on my left could be hiding anybody, but why hide? I'm frozen, expecting gunshot. Saba keeps munching.

I turn slowly, looking all around me. The sun is low, so there are shadows moving in the slight breeze from the branches of trees and bushes. I still can't see anything unusual. I begin to wonder if one of the keepers is trying something new without having asked about it. Some of them begin to think they know more about their particular animals than anybody, and they might have done something they considered harmless without having checked it out with me. I stand there breathing hard, afraid to move from what seems like a safe spot for the moment.

There's a cracking sound. I jerk and then realize that Saba has finished off most of the bundle and knocked the rest of it to the ground between us. I reach out to grab a piece to see what it is, but his huge head comes forward, his long curling eyelashes and fuzzy white muzzle inches from my face. I move my hand back, empty, and jump behind the tree, out of his reach. Although he looks soft and friendly, just curious, there's no confusion in my mind that he's a wild animal and I'm alone in his territory—I think.

I round the tree and run back to my truck. I pull on the door handle. The door doesn't budge. I look across and see that the passenger side is also locked. My keys are on the seat, where I left them. I don't remember locking the truck. I never lock it. I look around. Everything's dead quiet. If somebody else locked the truck, where could they be?

I check my watch. The park is closed now; it's past feeding time, near dark, so it's not likely I'll see any of the keepers driving down the road. I glance back inside the truck. My radio phone is on the seat. I'm faced with a walk back through giraffes, gemsbok, zebras, and rhinos before I can get to the gate and yell for somebody to let me out. I tell myself there shouldn't be a problem. I'll stay far enough away not to be threatening.

I start walking at a fast pace, coming out into the clear area so I can get a view and not come up on an animal suddenly. I'm thinking that the worst part will be the embarrassment when I get to the hospital and have to call somebody to give me a ride back out with my spare keys. I pass a couple gemsbok about thirty yards off. They give me a glance and put their heads down. I realize my scent is familiar out here, since I often drive with the truck window open. I'm hoping none of these guys links me up with a dart or a shot and decides to even out the relationship.

I'm wondering about the keeper who gave me the report. He's been employed here for a long time. Maybe I had a brain malfunction and locked the truck. The feed can be explained tomorrow.

I hear a noise behind me and turn. There are just a few zebras, drifting toward the water trough. I'm coming to a clump of trees. I can either go all the way around or take the shortcut through. I doubt any animals would be among the foliage now that the sun has gone down. I decide to go for it.

I step slowly into the dark of the ficus and holly trees and let my eyes rove over the nearest branches and hanging roots to check for spiders. Forget the fear, I tell myself; it's nothing compared to jumping out of an airplane. I move forward slowly along a sort of path made by the animals. I glance into the piles of leaves on the ground, shuffling a little to alert snakes, so they can scatter. I spot something—a glint of metal about six feet ahead. At first, I think it's a woven headband, mostly covered with leaves. I take a step closer and jerk back. There's something wrong. What I see is a loop of twisted wire. It doesn't belong here. Something I've read flashes into my mind—a trap—banned in certain parts of Africa. I recall a picture I saw in a wildlife magazine. I think. I can't be sure that I'm not dreaming this up, but I'm not going to test my guess.

I move far away to my left and walk fast off the path, taking the quickest route out. Forget the spiders. I duck through the hanging roots and keep my eyes focused on the leaves ahead. What the fuck is going on here? It's not paranoia. A foreign object has no way of getting out here unless somebody placed it. Could the thing have been there for years? It didn't look rusty. With the rugged walk through trees and brush, I'm breathing hard. Sweat is dripping into my eyes as I push aside the last branches and step out into a moonlit night. The beauty is unexpected, and I take a deep breath and lift my hair off my shoulders to catch the breeze. I stiffen as I see the outline of two rhinos standing silently about fifty yards to my left. Their tails are jerking up and down, so I know they're thinking something. I'm downwind, thank God, and dressed in dark green. I keep moving. If they've seen me, they're too bored to bother looking any closer.

I get to the road and stay on it for the last two hundred yards. I can see the spot where the gate is. Now, be there, I think. Let the guard be in the right place, doing his job. I cover those last few yards in seconds and throw off my pride, banging on the high wooden gate and yelling to be let out. After a few tries, I hear a reply, a voice asking who it is.

"It's Destiny," I answer. "Dr. Donne."

I hear footsteps on gravel, and finally there's the sound of keys opening the lock. The gate swings back and a young longhaired guy I don't recognize stares at me with his mouth open.

"Do you have ID?" he asks.

"No, I don't. I'm the vet here. My ID's in my office in the hospital. Who are you?"

He points at his uniform. "I'm a temp. The regular guy's out."

That's good, I think. He can give me a ride and won't be around to mention it to anybody else. Then a slant of light goes through my brain. "Have you let anybody else in or out tonight?"

He pauses, pulls on the scraggly beard on his chin. "No. Just one of the keepers."

"Who?"

"I don't remember the name. He had on a uniform, carrying a bale of hay. He forgot his keys, too."

"Hay?"

"Yeah. Feed."

"What did he look like?"

"Tall, light hair."

My breath catches. "What color eyes?"

"Shit. Sorry, Doctor. I dunno. Mustache."

I start breathing again. Couldn't be Tom if he doesn't remember the eyes. I must be losing my mind. Paranoia. "Would you mind getting a vehicle and taking me back out there? I had to leave my truck."

The guard follows me to unlock my office. It's all dark, and he waits till I flip on the light. I glance inside. I'm not going to be a whimp and have him walk me in. "I'll meet you at the truck. Thanks," I tell him.

I go in fast, throwing on the fluorescents in each of the three rooms. I get my spare keys from the desk drawer and grab a flash-light. I load up one of the Telinjects with a dose of tranquilizer. It can't hurt to be prepared. The guard will have to park behind me, and I won't be able to see much as I walk to the truck to unlock it. If anything or anybody sneaks up on me, I'll just stick 'em.

We drive out there, and I'm ashamed of myself. The night is so beautiful, and all the animals are quiet. The fresh scent of manure in the humid air is calming to me. I direct the guard to drive behind the trees and we pull up close to my truck. It's sitting exactly as I left it. Saba has moved on. No sign of him by the tree. I want to look for what he was eating, but there'd be no way of finding it in the dark. I'll get the explanation tomorrow.

When I finally get everything locked up for the night, it's nearly ten o'clock. I don't want to go home to my dark house, but I'm not comfortable popping in on Tom, either. I pass the only gas station for miles, and then think about going back to call, but it's a long, dark drive to his trailer and my dogs have to be let out. I haven't asked Corey to stop by.

It's ridiculous all the thinking I'm putting into this. I need to admit to myself that I stupidly locked the keys in the zebra, and nothing happened. The wires and the bale will be easily explained when I ask Gerald Path about it. Much ado about nothing. Miss Know-It-All in a panic.

I get home and force myself to walk in normally. No problem. I let the dogs out to run by themselves. Too bad if somebody complains. I can't wait to get on the phone with Tom. I dial his trailer number, but there's no answer. Nothing new. I leave a message, telling him to call me if he's home before eleven, because I need to get some sleep. I stop myself from thinking about him with Swan. I don't say to call me no matter how late, because I don't want to require an explanation, and I don't want to know if he doesn't go home. At 10:55, the gloom settles on me. I wonder if I should call back and say he can call up until midnight.

At five after eleven, the phone rings. The weight falls from my chest as I hear his voice. He says, sorry, he's been home all along, waiting to hear from me, and I must have called when he took out the trash. He finally checked the phone before he went to bed.

I don't question it. I tell him the story of my night. I make it light because it sounds so silly now, but he doesn't think so. I can hear the worry. The serious tone scares me again. "I'm sure I'll get a full explanation in the morning," I tell him. "It doesn't make sense anyway. It's a risky way to try to kill me. How could they be sure anything would happen?"

"What if somebody made a false report, lured the giraffe out there, and set a trap for you?"

"They couldn't be sure I'd cut through that patch of trees."

"Who knows what might've been waiting in the other direction."

His words send a quick chill down my back, but I don't give in to it. "It's too much trouble. They could get me more easily."

"Maybe she's enjoying the terrorizing—the stalking and building up of your fear. Revenge to soothe her ego."

"I don't know. It's too crazy."

"I don't think you should mention anything about this to the park people."

"Why not?"

"The police. They're bound to call 'em."

"I have to get somebody to remove that trap, or whatever it is, before some animal wanders into it. I don't know how it works."

"When can you go?" he asks.

"Huh?"

"I'll meet you there as soon as you can make it. I'll get that sucker out."

"You might hurt yourself."

"Fuck. No problem. I'm handy."

Tom is waiting in the parking lot at one o'clock the next day, as planned. I admire his shining golden hair and perfect proportions as I walk toward him. I never would have expected to be involved with such a physically beautiful human being, pure animal perfection.

"Hi, sweetheart," he says. "No students this afternoon, so I have plenty of time." He pulls me to him for a kiss that buckles my knees. I wonder if anybody's watching. As he pulls back, he lifts the hair off my neck. "You doin' okay?"

"Now I am."

He puts his arm around my shoulder and we walk across the grass to where my zebra is parked. "We'll take care of it."

I park in the area next to the clump of trees. "Hold on," I tell him. I get out and look around. No animals nearby. I motion to Tom and he comes around beside me. I think about my keys but leave them on the seat. I'm not going to let paranoia change my life.

We walk into the dense shady area and I stay in front of Tom and move slowly, trying to locate the contraption among the low ferns and vines. I make my way through the area where I remember it was, but there's nothing. I keep walking to the clearing, although I know it can't be that far.

"Don't move," I tell Tom. "It's not where I thought. I must have gotten my directions mixed up."

He nods. He's standing with his arms crossed, patient, his eyes roving through the brush to my right.

I turn ninety degrees to the left and make my slow search again all the way to the clearing, then walk back to Tom. "I thought it was right here."

"It probably was." He points to where I saw him staring. "It looks to me like somebody's already picked it up."

I look into the underbrush. There are some crushed ferns and vines. I follow the vines to a couple broken branches on a low holly tree. "A gemsbok or zebra could have done that."

"Could've," he says, "but a gemsbok didn't remove the trap. We've got our answer—unless you're just loony." He smiles.

I shake my head. "Not sure."

He says he'll be careful and help me finish the search. No sense him standing there. We sweat our asses off and don't find anything.

We walk back toward the truck. "I wish I knew more about that trap—if that's what it was. I don't know what they were trying to do."

"Scare you good. Or with a little luck, maybe kill you."

"Why?"

"I don't know how to make this real to you. You haven't been raised on self-indulgence—there's no limit."

We reach the truck and get in. The keys are still there, thank God. I grab a couple of paper towels and hand them to Tom, take one myself and wipe my face. "I'm going to have to talk to security. How are these people getting in and out of the park?"

"I'd say somebody who works here is getting paid. They're not going to tell you anything."

I let out a whoosh of air. "I don't know what to do."

"We'll figure it out," he says. He takes my face in his hands and makes me look into his eyes. "Okay, sweetheart?"

I nod.

"We'll figure it out."

chapter

NINETEEN

me stay calm by phoning in the afternoons and spending the nights at my house. He's decided that our being together isn't going to make any difference at this point, since she's already gone to the extreme. He'd rather be around to protect me. I haven't come to any conclusions. I've become a follower. I just keep working hard and pushing the fear out of my mind. If I lose my job, it's my life anyway. I won't jeopardize the animals' health. If I'm my responsible self, chaos can burn itself out around me.

Saturday afternoon, I get out in time to head over to the DZ to catch a jump. A freefall releases all my tension, at least for a while. I can die of only one thing, so I'll choose. Gravity is much more predictable than this woman I've never met. I feel safe at the DZ. Everybody knows everybody, so people can't go wandering around without notice. A tight throat and fluttering stomach for a few minutes are easily repaid with the rush afterward.

Tom is surprised to see me so early, but he seems pleased. He gives me a kiss at the hangar door, and I start to relax right away—until he tells I'm due to transition from the student rig with the ripcord to the throw-out pilot chute. Any new unknown this point is a source of heightened fear. He takes me into the packing area and shows me the little chute, about a two-foot diameter of nylon and mesh on a six-foot strap called the bridle. He folds the chute up into a hot dog shape and tucks it into the bottom of the rig. It has a short plastic pipe just like a ripcord that sticks out of the pocket. He explains that when the air catches the chute, it yanks the pin and pulls out the main. He puts the rig on me and tells me how to throw it out. After a couple of practice tries, I toss it away fine. Nonetheless, I know he reads the look of terror on my face.

"Perfect. Do a few more," he tells me. He puts his arm around my shoulder and pats my arm. It's nice, but I'm not comforted.

"Just make sure you're good and stable when you throw, so you don't catch the bridle somewhere on your arm or leg. If you hang on to it and it wraps around your wrist, you can cause a horseshoe malfunction. Think of it like a snake—throw it away fast."

I try to smile convincingly. "I like snakes."

He chuckles. "I should have known."

"What if I get a horseshoe malfunction?"

"If you throw like you just did, you won't."

"But what if I—"

"Shake it off, or if you can't, cut away and pull the reserve. The main is only an accessory; the reserve is the one you count on. Hopefully, the main will clear so you don't get the canopies tangled."

I look at him and bite my lip. "If they entangle, I'm close to Grandma, right?"

"Get off it. Not necessarily. You might have enough canopy up to slow your descent. At that point, you try to fly it—you can deal with a lot of things if you don't panic." He looks at me.

I nod to the double meaning. "I just like to be informed."

He pauses and touches his finger to his lip. "Oh, also, there's no computer on the one-ninety rental. But there's no reason you'd need one. You're not going to be jumping with anyone to bang into and go unconscious. You'll do fine."

I take a deep breath. I won't be a wimp. "Yeah. Okay."

He looks into me with those blues. "I know you can handle it, but if you want, I'll jump with you for this first one."

My nervousness drops several notches. "Sure. You know I'd like that."

"I'll stay to the side and make sure you open." He tells me to get a rig from Lee while he goes to manifest us.

He comes back in a couple minutes with my rental slip. He has a tandem on the next load and we're on the load after that.

I take my rig off the rack and over to the couch on the far side of the hangar so that nobody else will use it. Tom gets his rig and comes over beside me.

"You need to get your altimeter from manifest—sorry, I should have brought one back with me." He gives me a peck. "See you in a few," he says. He turns to get his rig and I head over to pick up my altimeter.

There's a line to sign up, so I have to wait a few minutes to get my altimeter. When I get back, Tom's just heading out of the hangar on the far side. There's a small group walking together in front of him, including a petite blond cutie in a harness, so I figure she's his tandem, the most attractive one, as usual. No doubt it pleases the girls to have his pretty face on their videos.

I go back to the couch to do a gear check while I'm waiting. I look over the front, checking all the mechanisms, as I've been taught: ring in a ring, cables fine on the cutaway, reserve handle tucked in good. I turn the container over and look at the back, see that the throw-out is stuffed neatly into the pocket, with the plastic handle showing. Check the pin. It's fine. No computer to look at, but that's no problem—Tom will be there.

The announcement to be at the plane in ten minutes comes over the speaker, and I make a dash to the ladies' room to relieve the usual churning in my guts. I know it's an effect of the norepinephrine running through my system, the flight-or-fight hormone. I'm ready to fly all right. I wonder if someday my guts will cool, if I'll live long enough to become comfortable. I go to the locker to put on the jumpsuit Dolly has loaned me, then dash across the building to borrow a helmet and goggles from the rental gear.

Jumpers are landing as I walk outside, but I don't see Tom. When I go back inside the hangar, he's already there, shrugging his rig onto his shoulders. Must have landed first and come through the other side.

I hear the Porter and follow Tom out the door. We climb into the plane with the others and belt in. I breathe from my diaphragm and let the deep breaths out slowly to relax as we climb. At intervals, I check my altimeter, trying to guess what altitude we're at. It's good to learn, I'm told, and gives me something to do besides obsess on what could go wrong. Tom's sitting behind me, and I twist far enough to smile at him. He's lost in thought until I catch his eye. He winks.

My nerves reach their peak as somebody calls, "Door," and opens it to that vast blue. Dano calls, "Cut," and he climbs out on the wing, ready to do video. Kathy, Vicki, Debbie, Cindy, Sandy, and Caroline, the regular women jumpers, wearing teddies and lace panties, two in garter belts, position themselves near the door, laughing, skin covered with goose bumps. It's a lingerie jump, with video—something I can wait for until my landing skills are dependable. I've seen video of nude jumps—an added thrill— lots of exposure if you break a leg, or worse. They take grips and move in unison to the call of "Ready, set, go"—they're gone.

My breathing is heavy with fear, but I do a crouching walk to the door and set myself backward as planned, holding the rail above me, my legs on the outside step, one foot trailing in the wind. I'm ready. Fear snaps into excitement. If I could see my eyes, I know they'd have sparks flying out of them. Tom takes the grips on my upper arms and we're out.

We stabilize instantly, falling together with arms locked, looking into each other's eyes. I feel a contented grin take up my face. Then in a gentle move, Tom pulls us together and kisses me—

twelve thousand feet, zooming toward earth at 125 mph, or more, terminal velocity, and I'm higher on the warmth of his mouth, locked to his lips. Fearless. What else is life for? He pulls back and shows me the altimeter on his hand—a two-thousand-foot kiss. There's plenty of time left, so he slips his hands down to my wrists and shows me how to move, arching his body more to fall faster, cupping to slow down. Speed is imperceptible, but I can see his level changing in respect to mine. At six thousand feet, he gives me a quick kiss good-bye and moves to the side so I can wave off and throw my pilot chute.

I bring my hands together over my head to signal, then reach down to find the small plastic pipe. I whip it out and away. Nothing happens. Nothing. I look to the side, and there's no pilot chute. A stinging shock goes through my body. I'm suddenly aware of the speed as I head toward earth, still hard in my arch. I find my reserve handle and grab it, give it a yank. It comes out in my hand, a foot or so of cable. Nothing happens. I look over my shoulder, thinking there's a burble. Nothing's out! The altimeter grows large to my eyes, 2,800 feet. I'm one in millions—a double malfunction . . . double malfunction. I think of Tom, but I don't see him. Solid calm comes over me and I feel the wind on my arms and legs. I forgive the rigger, think of my mother—sorry—

I feel a touch and realize Tom has docked on my side. I turn my head and stare into his glittering eyes, thinking he's going down with me, giving up his life rather than leave me alone. His teeth are gritted eerily, his cheeks pulled back by the wind. "No," I yell. Then he's gone. I'm alone, icy, numb.

There's a jerk, and I look up. In a supernatural slowing of time, my eyes focus on the vibrating bauble of fabric hovering above my head. As I watch, unfeeling, the nylon poufs and unfurls a rainbow—fluorescent, shining, tranquil, my colors spread flat and wide above me. I'm snug in the hold of safety.

Tom is already below me, to my right, his blues against the

green field. I look at my altimeter, less than five hundred feet, a short time to set up a landing. I steel myself to stop shaking. I follow Tom, do a crosswind turn, then into the wind. In seconds, it's time to flare, a long, even pull on the toggles. I feel the stall, and the field comes up solid under my feet. I hop a little forward and run it out. It's my first stand-up landing. I laugh out loud—or maybe it's a cry.

I pull in a toggle to get my canopy settled on the ground and drop my helmet and goggles, take a breath. Reality hits: a double malfunction. I should be slopped like a fresh egg on the grass, a puddle of broken bones, burst organs, and running fluids.

My legs go to jelly just as Tom walks up, drops his chute to the side, and reaches out to pull me into his body. He squeezes me hard and I feel the metal buckle of his chest strap bite into my shoulder. It feels good. "How's that for timing?" he asks. He's exhilarated.

I cling to him. I begin to laugh and sob, dry sobs, but the feeling of relief is wild.

We stand there for minutes. He holds me, stroking down the back of my head, and I shake with blubbering hysteria. Looking over his shoulder, I see the others landing in the expert field, calm, as if nothing had happened.

"Come on," he says. He takes my face and kisses me. "Easy. We don't want to draw attention."

"What?" I swipe my arm across my nose and wipe my face.

"C'mon." He picks up his canopy and starts walking. I manage to wad mine into my arms and get my legs working. He stops for me to catch up. "We don't have to explain. I can do the repairs for you—I'm certified."

"What are you talking about?" I stop and wait for him to step back to me. "You want me to keep this a secret?"

He lets out a loud breath. "I'll explain it all to you, but you can't say a word. I told you we can't bring in the police—unless you want to get me put in prison."

"The police? You mean this was an attempt to kill me?"

"Let's keep moving while we talk. I don't want Dolly and the girls watching out the window and wondering if we're having a problem."

I feel my heart beating hard, and I can barely hear Tom above the noise in my ears. "This was no accident," he says. "Somebody cut the bridle on the pilot chute and—I would bet—clipped the reserve cable inside the container. If I hadn't been with you, and able to yank the bridle, you'd be dead."

"No. That's impossible. How'd they know I'd take that rig?"

"Waited till he saw you with it—just seconds with a knife and clippers."

"Somebody cut the bridle on purpose?"

He reaches into my bundle of nylon and pulls out the piece of black strap. The end isn't frayed or chewed. The cut is clean. "Yes, sweetheart, and reserve cable. Pure sabotage. A clever job of it." His breathing is loud in my ear. "I'll have to take a took around for that pilot chute. Probably went into the cane, but we don't want anybody else to find it." He stuffs the empty bridle back into the bundle. "There'd be no way to spot that unless you were suspicious and opened up the rig."

"How did you fix it?"

"I didn't fix it. I used your bridle like a static line, so when I opened, I yanked out your canopy."

The facts are sinking in. I'm beginning to shake. "I didn't see anybody hanging around."

"Neither did I, but I have a good idea who it was."

"Who?"

"Roth."

"Roth? He hasn't been around since the accident, has he?"

"I should have made fucking sure of that. He's the only one who could have done this."

"Why would he?"

"Swan's brother? He'd do it for her, the lovely Swan."

His tone is so dark that it scares me, in spite of the condition I'm already in. Tom is almost admitting to have caused Roth's accident, and he's blaming him for my attempted murder. Swan's brother. I try to keep up the pace and put everything out of my mind. If only I can hold up long enough to get back to the hangar. That's as far as I can think.

"No doubt somebody saw how low we opened, and word'll get around. Let me answer the questions."

"I don't see how you can keep this quiet."

"Don't worry. People know better than to piss me off. I'll tell 'em that you held on to the pilot chute too long—easy thing to happen your first time. It got wrapped around your arm, and I had to cut it off and help you open—just how I did it, in fact."

"So I have to play the fool."

"It's easy to make that mistake when you're used to holding the ripcord."

"You carry a knife in the air?"

"Sure, a hook knife. Everybody does—the experienced people." He unsnaps a small pocket on his chest strap and pulls out an orange plastic hook with an X-Acto–type blade nestled inside the curve.

"Should I get one of those?"

"Wait till you know what to do with it." He laughs and puts his hand on my arm. "Never made a stand-up landing before, did you?"

"Nope. That was my first."

He winks. "That means you buy tonight—case of beer—skydiver tradition."

"Forget it," I say. I laugh in spite of everything. He can lighten my mood, no matter what. "I'm good under pressure."

"So am I," he says.

"Oh, Tom, I'm so sorry. You saved my life and I didn't even say thank you."

"Silly girl. I saved you for me. You owe me big-time." He presses his face against mine. Warmth spreads through my chest. "Just concentrate on telling people about your stand-up and forget all the rest. There won't be any more attempts here. I'll make sure of that. Besides, they know we're onto their game."

I wince at his calling an attempt on my life a game again, but I let it go.

"Smile," he says as we get within a few yards of the hangar. "Keep on walking straight into my office and leave your rig there."

Everybody is busy packing on the floor and nobody says anything as we walk past. I look around for Roth. I'm sure I would have seen him if he'd been in the hangar. Tom wants him to be the one. If Roth was around, somebody had to have seen him.

When we get to the office I take off my parachute and strip off my jumpsuit. A disabling fatigue comes over me and I slump into Tom's chair.

Tom opens the door of the adjoining classroom and looks to see if anybody's there, then comes back and stands over me, his hands lifting my face. "Something has to be done. This wasn't an attempt to scare you. It was a plan for your death."

I take his wrists and move his hands to my shoulders. "You're right." I reach for the phone. "I'm calling the police."

He grips my arm. "You're going to have to trust me. The police can't guard you night and day. You'd just be causing me a lot of trouble—and look what it would do to Caleb's business."

"Caleb's business?"

"Yeah, a sabotage investigation might scare away a few customers from jumping here, don't you think?

"I'm sorry, for Christ's sake, but I'm not responsible for any of this."

"No? You knew I was married early on."

My head is spinning. I didn't know he was still seeing his wife—until when? Not until he'd done everything he could to make me fall in love. How could I have known where all this would lead? He'd lied.

"Look, if it'd save your life, we'd take our chances, no matter what, and call the police. But it wouldn't work. How can the police protect you? You gonna sit around your house twenty-four/seven with a guard?" He looks hard at me. "There's only one way you'll be safe."

"What?"

"Think about it."

"Split up?"

He shakes his head, looks at me, shakes it again. "I doubt that matters anymore."

"Then what?"

His eyes aim like lasers. "You tell me."

I lurch out of the chair, heading toward the door, refusing to think anymore. "Last load is down. I'm going to get a beer from DZ Mom." I turn back to face him. "I don't know what world you're living in."

"Don't say anything to DZ Mom about this."

WHEN I GET TO HER SCREENED kitchen, Mom's already heard from Jacques about the low opening. She hands me a Busch Light and I sit on one of her stools and tell her I'm not sure what the problem was. "Basically, I guess I panicked," I say. I change the subject to Ginger, her dog, and Lucky, the DZ dog owned by Kenny, the airport caretaker. I mention that I heard they'd mated and ask if it's true Ginger is twelve years old. I tell Mom I'll be happy to take a look at Ginger—at her age, a pregnancy could be dangerous. I can tell Mom's looking at me with a purpose, but she doesn't push it.

When I see Tom walking toward his car, I throw my empty beer can in the trash. He's waiting to follow me home—my house tonight, as arranged. I tell Mom thanks. As I close the door, I notice she has a full view of the entrance gate. I holler back through the screen. "Forgot—I was looking for Roth. Have you seen him today?"

She looks at me. Her eyes also happen to be a keen blue, though not so electric as Tom's. "No, hon, haven't seen him since the accident." There's a question in her tone.

I yell, "Thanks" on the run and don't turn back. I get into my car for the torturous ride with my thoughts. Tom pulls out ahead—I guess I'm following. I wonder how I'm going to make it all the way alone. I'm tired and I need to talk things out—although he's made it clear the talking is done. I keep my eyes on his Bronco and try to convince myself he's all wrong about Swan's intentions.

It seems like hours till I pull up to the house behind Tom. Instantly, I get a good feeling, despite myself. He goes around back while I'm getting my jumpsuit and stuff together.

He's waiting on the porch. "You should give me a key," he says.

I hand him the keys.

He looks at me quizzically. "I'm glad you still have your sense of humor."

"I wasn't thinking," I say. I start laughing loud as it hits me that he meant a key to keep, not my keys at the moment. I know it isn't that funny, and I'm a little over the edge into hysteria. He grabs me and shuts me up with his mouth and his tongue. His hands are firm behind my head. He pulls me aside and puts the key in the lock.

"Yeah," I say, "better get me inside before I disturb the neighborhood." I'm kidding, but Tom doesn't laugh. "I have an extra key I'll give you," I tell him. "I don't know why I didn't think of it before."

We walk in and the kids start wiggling their tail ends. He pats both heads. "You're naturally cautious. That's fine." He looks at me.

"I'm tired of it."

Tom leans against the counter and tells me he was right. He didn't want to ask too many questions, but Lee, the rigger, talked to Roth in the hangar. "He wasn't there long, just picked up his reserve repack from the day of the accident. That's odd—having Lee do the repack. Roth is a rigger himself."

I'm thinking the odd part is that DZ Mom didn't see Roth—but then, she must be busy cooking most of the time. "He might still be on pain killers."

"Whatever. Anyway, he was here when your rig was tampered with. Proof enough for me."

"Do Swan and Roth know you're involved in the lion cub business?"

"Oh yeah. They're the ones got me started."

"So they know you'll talk me out of calling the police. They feel perfectly safe right now."

"Probably."

I put my palms to my head, try to keep the brains from exploding. "This whole thing—I can't deal with it."

He puts his hand on the back of my neck and massages. "I'm here for you. We're together. I'll help you—whatever you want to do. You're smart enough to figure this out—we're genius together."

My throat is tight. All my life, people have been telling me how smart I am, usually when they want something done. Now my own life depends on making an intelligent decision, and I'm totally incapable, haven't been able to think for weeks.

The kids come up and lick my fingers, sensing my stress. Of course, they want their dinner. I go to the closet and fill the dog bowls with dry food. When I turn back, Tom's gone off into another room. I give the kids some fresh water, feeling my body begin to tingle with the expectation of Tom's breath and skin and cock. I know I'm insane—it doesn't take long until the threats against me seem like far-off clouds suspended without movement.

He's naked, spread-eagle on the sheets and staring at the ceiling fan, when I get to the bedroom. "Hot in here," he says. He props his head. "Get your clothes off, sweets."

I yank my T-shirt over my head and throw off my bra, unzip my shorts, and step out of both pants at once. I'm ready to lose myself, let my body and mind go out of control in the heat and sweat and steady movement I can depend on. I flop down beside him, and Tom rolls over and puts his mouth on mine. His body pins me to the bed, solid against me. It's what I need.

He lifts his head and stares at me. I can feel his eyes, but it's too dark to see. I would have imagined they'd light the room. "Don't worry. I'm going to help you," he says. He works down my body and I feel his fingers prying me apart and his firm, wet tongue vibrating against my clitoris. He's helping already. I sink into myself, choosing pure sensation as my reality, no fear, no other needs. He moves his face back to mine and glides his cock into the hot, moist gap I offer up. I tilt my pelvis, squeezing my muscles for a slow, hard pull, the slippery friction that drags my mind right out of my body. I know I'm a pure fool, and I don't care.

In the morning when I wake up, Tom's gone. I can't believe I've slept straight through. I reach for my eyedrops on the nightstand and lubricate. There's a sheet of paper next to the clock. I pick it up and heat rushes over me—a love letter or a good-bye? It's neither. A map—the directions to a destination west of Palm Beach—marked with an X. On the bottom of the sheet, he's printed "Swan's horse farm." My chest tightens up. What does he expect me to do, drive over there and shoot her?

I get into the shower automatically, shaking my head in wonder. I drop the shampoo, and the bottle hits my toe hard. Not my day. Trying to wash my face, I jam my little finger up my nose and cut the inside with my fingernail. It bleeds. I can't live like this, disabled by fear. Yet it still doesn't feel real that she's tried to kill me—twice. I can't conceive of someone with the money and ability to have someone killed—only happens in books or movies. Then again, Tom is high stakes. I can understand the feverish, insane desire to eliminate barriers to him. I feel it myself when I imagine he's with her. Watching him walk the beautiful girls to the plane, the ones he straps close to his body and escorts into the blue, makes me uncomfortable. They're all flirting with him. He can do whatever he wants. If he meets them later, I'll never find out.

I stand under the hot water and try to imagine how Swan must feel if she's still in love with him. If she has the power to eliminate me from his life and not even participate, why not? I dry off, wondering what kind of a body she's got. Probably tall and lean—can eat whatever she wants—with fine, flawless skin. With her money, she's always had the best of care and nutrition, health spas to keep in shape, plastic surgery if some part of her body wasn't perfect. I remember Tom's comment about my breasts being real. The Palm Beach set—I don't know a thing about them.

I go back into the bedroom and pick up the map. The place should be easy to find. Tom must figure they're not following me during the day, or he wouldn't have left the map. I'll just take a look around. Doing something will help me, instead of sitting and waiting for her to make another attempt on my life.

I reach into the drawer to find my darkest pair of glasses. I put them on and look at myself in the mirror, pin up my hair. It falls back down. I pull off the glasses and drop them on the dresser. This is ridiculous. Am I really going to disguise myself and case someone's property? I stand there paralyzed, blank. I want to go, see what kind of wealth he's talking about. I can't take my car over there. I'm sure to be recognized. What could Tom have been thinking to leave that map? Maybe he knows something about Swan's schedule to send me there, but I don't want to take that chance.

I call Corey and ask if I can switch cars with her. I tell her I have a long drive to a patient's farm and I'm afraid of a recurring overheating problem. She's home for the day and only needs to drive five minutes to the grocery, so she's fine with the idea. I put the glasses back on and stare at myself. I have a wig in the closet left over from a Halloween party, in case Swan has seen photos of me. In the movies, a private eye would take photos, and that's the feeling I have right now. I realize that I've just told a lie. I can do this.

SWAN'S HORSE FARM IS EASY TO find, east between the Florida Turnpike, and State Road 7, a short distance south. Once I pass the turnpike, I know I'm close. It's a horse community, vast acreage, neatly fenced, houses and stables discreetly set back from the road behind ornately iron-gated brick walls. I smell the sweetness of the horses, one of my great loves, yet I feel like I've crossed a boundary into a country where I don't belong. Miss Superior, too sophisticated, too educated for Pahokee, is now on the downside of snobbery—literally on the other side of the fence—riding the fringes of the invisible people, the out-of-sight rich, who don't put their names on mailboxes, don't want their property or wealth known. The more outsiders know, the more wealth becomes a liability, the golden life that others believe they deserve to take. But I'm here to protect myself—nothing else.

I pass a number on the right. I'm almost there. The jitters come over me. I slow down and push my glasses back on my head to gaze into a deep grove of ficus shading half a dozen horses a hundred yards from the road, some muscular thoroughbreds and quarter horses, dark, shining bays and chestnuts, white stockings bright in the shadows. I pull onto the shoulder of the road. There's one white pasofino, the sleek neck high and regal with the curve of his Arabian ancestry. He stands out among the group, delicate, but with an erect bearing, slapping his tail occasionally, nonchalantly, as if he has it all figured out, the smallest effort to keep the annoying flies off his velvety coat. The breed is said to carry a rider with a glass of wine on his head, never spilling a drop. He takes a few steps and there's the proud strut of the Tennessee walker, a show horse among the runners. The horse turns to nip some grass and I see it's a female.

An icy clamp compresses my chest. This horse is the swan among the ugly ducklings, despite the rich beauty and grace of the others. A shining white-blond, taller than the rest, the posture of healthy self-assurance, taut with energy, darting an alert eye. My mind crowds with images of her, Swan, surrounded by herself, collections of pale and delicate figurines, original Audubons, snowy sofas and satin down comforters, thick cream carpets and milky lace window treatments. Outside is her baby, her posturing double. The two of them can strut—Swan, tailored and slim, in white riding habit and helmet, a blond ponytail bouncing, crop tucked under her arm.

I know the next gate will have her number. I glance at the map—yes, on the left. I take my foot off the brake and pull back onto the pavement, drive slowly. It wasn't a good idea coming here. What did I expect to do, climb over the fence and jog up to the stalls to meet her? I try to let go of her image, but it becomes more vivid. I imagine her with a dimple, like the one my old roommate had. She rode in jumping events, a gorgeous girl. She'd been thrown and landed on her face, and when she healed, she had a dimple. She was more beautiful than before.

I'll drive by Swan's gate and go home, tell Tom I'm tired of acting like a fool. It's time to go to the police.

As I approach the drive that should be hers, a sweat comes over me. The gate is open, the only one on the road. The number is correct. I pass by. My mind swirls with possibilities. It seems to be fate—I'm supposed to go inside. I look at my face in the rearview mirror. She can't recognize me, red hair and lots of makeup, big sunglasses, sun hat—a small-town tourist who doesn't realize people don't stop in to say howdy.

I back up into the grass and turn around. I pull in and drive slowly down the smooth blacktop. A luxurious lawn spreads out broad and long in front of me—nice place for a landing if you needed one. I roll down the window and catch the scent of orange blossoms on a light breeze. A long white building comes into view from behind the trees. These are obviously stalls; otherwise, I would think it's a house, so beautifully kept, a graceful old style that fits alongside the spreading banyan trees as if it grew there with them. Deep ruby bougainvilleas hug the white walls, clean colors against the blue sky.

The driveway continues on to what must be the house, but I turn in front of the stable. No one's in sight to stop me. Certainly no worries about security around here. The heavy door is ajar. I park on the drive and get out quickly, then make myself slow down. I walk idly toward the door, looking all around and keeping my arms loose at my sides, as though I couldn't be more relaxed on such a wonderful day.

"Hello, anybody here?" I call. My voice is shaky. I pull the door open just far enough to step inside. My breath goes out in wonder. The stable is all fine wood and shining brass, totally air-conditioned. The clean smell of alfalfa and horse soap takes me back to the stables at the University of Kentucky, where I spent a couple of undergraduate years. I'd often taken my books to the stables to study among my favorite friends. A horse nickers down the row and one puts his head over the stall gate near my shoulder to study me with his huge compassionate eye.

I'm startled as a door creaks at the end stall. A thin dark-haired woman in jeans and a T-shirt steps out from the far right. "Can I help you?" She has a curry comb in her hand, and I realize she's been grooming the full leopard Appaloosa that tries to follow her out. She turns and strokes his mane, moving him back as she shuts the gate. My knees are wobbly.

I walk toward her, the scuff of my sandals on the plank flooring loud in the silence. She isn't a bit suspicious, obviously used to people dropping in. She's not so formidable as I expected—not anything like I expected.

I center myself. "I hope you don't mind—it's such a beautiful place. I just wanted to stick my head in and take a look." As I get close, I see she has splotches of paint on her clothes, several colors, loose jeans. She's pretty in a quiet way, maybe a couple years older than I am. Particles of sawdust cling to her knees from where she must have been kneeling in the stall.

She wipes sweat off her forehead with the back of her hand, gathers her dark hair behind her neck. "No problem," she says. "The gate's open for some high school girls who come here to ride. Thought you might be one of them—late—wanting to saddle up."

My mind is making a turn. She's normal and down-to-earth, nothing like Tom described. I motion around the stable. "I love horses—"

The door opens wide and she turns. A younger woman walks in, brisk and haughty. I feel a stiffness come into my neck. She's a beautiful blonde, white riding helmet above fluffy curls, tailored beige coat fitted lightly to her athletic proportions. Her soft leather boots tap firmly as she strides toward us, not a hint of perspiration on her face or a wrinkle in her jodphurs. She looks straight at me and turns to the other woman. "Meet me at the house. I'm going up to have some lunch."

"Okay. Five minutes? I'll just finish with Chips."

The blonde nods, turns, and clips back out, without a hi or bye, and without acknowledging my existence. I feel a drop of sweat run between my breasts. I realize I'd been holding my breath. Now the details fit. She's the perfect rich girl, with every personality detail that Tom has implied. I've seen her and I'll never forget her. She's more striking than my imagination was able to create.

The groomer puts her hand lightly on my forearm, and I can see an apology in her eyes for the rudeness that she was forced to take part in. "I need to finish and lock up. Sorry you didn't get much of a look around."

I feel disgusted and sympathetic that she has to put up with this kind of attitude to make a living. "Oh, no. I'm sorry. I shouldn't have walked in. It's great just to see the inside of a place like this." I start walking and wave. "Thanks. Take care."

"Come back earlier sometime if you'd like to ride."

"Thank you. I'm just here on vacation. But thanks so much." I slip through the door and walk quickly toward my car. There's no sign of Swan. I figure she's at the house having foie gras and caviar, watercress soup—a simple lunch. I wonder why she was in such a hurry. Then it hits me. She could have recognized my assistant's car. I was foolish to drive it right onto her property. She probably came into the stable just to get a look at me and then called the groomer away so I couldn't hang around and ask questions.

I get into the car and start it, try not to floor it down the drive. I pass the gate with relief and turn onto the road. Maybe I'm just paranoid and she didn't notice, or doesn't know the car after all. She wouldn't be following me personally. The hired help would do that. But I'll have to tell Tom and see what he thinks. I don't know what it might mean if she knows I was at her place in disguise.

I return the car immediately and wrestle with my fears the rest of the day, trying to decide why Tom sent me there in the first place, and why I went. So now I know what she looks like. I've seen her demanding attitude and complete dismissal of others. She's a good match to Tom in looks. I can't help think what good-looking children they'd have together. Of course, she was willing to move out of her circle to bring him in, but then she couldn't change him into the doting puppy that she had envisioned.

Around eight, I hear Tom's truck in the drive and drop my wineglass. It breaks on the tiled kitchen floor. I'm off balance. I've had this jittery feeling before, while waiting to get on the plane, but not so bad. I'm afraid of what he's going to say.

As I'm picking up glass and kicking the big pieces out of the dogs' way, he uses his key to open the door. Despite the aggressive affection launched at him by Clue and Angel, his eyes sweep over the mess. He steps to my side. I feel myself ready to collapse as his arm comes around me and he picks the shards from my hand and sets them on the counter. He takes my hand to the faucet and sluices the particles from between my fingers. I've been barely keeping myself together all day, and now that he's here, the wires of my stress snap. He holds my weight against him. The need for tears throbs in my head.

"You okay, sweetheart? Okay?"

"I saw her. She's just like you said."

"Swan? You went over there? I didn't expect you to go over there."

I look at him. He's startled. "I thought that's why you left the map."

"I thought you'd call me first to talk about it—find out a good time." He puts a hand to his forehead. "Never dreamed you'd drive right over there, hon. That was dangerous. What did you do?"

"I didn't go there to do anything. Just look around. I'm okay. I wore a wig. She didn't recognize me."

His eyebrows go up. He smiles. "I'm amazed. I didn't know you—"

"Fuck. I jump out of planes, don't I? I have some guts—and a little bit of sense."

He nods. "How'd you get inside?"

"The gate was open."

"No shit. What did you talk about?"

"We didn't talk. I talked to an older woman grooming the horses. She was nice."

His brows knit. "Wait a sec. Tell me this from the beginning."

I gave him the play-by-play, including how Swan rudely ignored me and spoke so curtly to the other woman.

Tom chews his lip as he listens. "Where'd you park?"

I grit my teeth. "You're making me nervous."

"Sorry, everything's okay." He kisses me. "She saw your car?"

"No, I drove Corey's. But she might know it, too. I didn't think of that until later."

"Sweetheart . . . I would say so. She'd have a full report, if she hasn't seen it herself."

"There are a million cars like that."

He shakes his head. "Yeah, but they don't turn up on her property. She's no dummy. I bet that's why she stopped in at the stable. You're lucky she didn't catch you alone in there."

"What could she do? She's not physically threatening."

"Did she have her shoulder bag?"

"I don't know. No, she looked like she'd just dismounted."

"Well, she carries a gun—a real one, not a tranquilizer gun."

"She wouldn't shoot me in her own stable anyway. It'd scare the horses."

"Okay, but you get my point. You took a chance."

The air goes out of me. "Living is taking a chance."

He folds me into his arms, squeezes my head against his chest like he would a child. I breathe in the clean fragrance of his shirt and feel his warmth through it on my face. I just want to stay there.

"I don't know what she'll do now. She won't like the idea of you checking out her territory."

I roll my face back and forth slowly against his shirt, feeling the soft cotton, his strong chest. I talk into him without lifting my head. "I can't take this anymore. I can't. I can't keep going through this."

I barely hear his words through the sounds of my own weeping and the noise of his shirt rubbing across my ears. "We're going to have to do something then. The two of us. Together."

Tom takes my head and stops the movement, pushes me back,

looks me in the eyes. I know he sees fear—and guilt. I do want her gone—just gone—but she's never going to leave. He lifts me behind the knees and carries me into the bedroom. He settles me on the bed and puts his lips to my neck, kissing his way down the plane of my chest. I feel frozen, nothing, but he doesn't stop. He rubs his face into me like a furry animal. He reaches down and pulls up my shirt, throws it off, unfastens my bra in front and strips it back. My nipples are erect with the chill. He moves down and takes both of them into his mouth.

"She's beautiful, picture-perfect," I tell him. My voice is pleading for him to say it's not true, to help me understand why he's giving her up, going for me.

His short nails tighten on my breasts until I squirm. He raises his face and his blue lasers penetrate my brain. "She's evil. You hear me? Evil. Think of your body broken on the ground, blood running, head cracked open—your eyes burst out of their sockets from the impact. That's the picture she wanted of you."

He lets go of me and comes down over my mouth, covering me completely with his body, kissing hard, cupping my ears and blocking out the world until I'm wrapped in his heat and conformed to his muscle and bone. He lifts his head and rolls to the side. "We'll go away for a few days—a week. There's a boogie at Lake Wales, an hour's drive or so, lots of planes—no Swan. Jump your ass off. There's a group going from here, and DZ Mom is taking her kitchen."

"I can't get off work."

"Think about it. Ever seen it on a gravestone that the person wished he'd spent more hours on the job?"

He's chilling me. "My job is my life. It's not just work."

He bends and kisses me on the throat. "I kinda thought I was your life—at least a good part of it." He tilts my face up. I try to smile.

I HAVE A FEW APPOINTMENTS
scheduled for the week, but nothing that can't be postponed. I call
Gerald Path at the park and tell him that I have a family emergency
and need to go home for a few days. He says he can handle the
urgent treatments, no problem. I figure I'll just work extra hours to
catch up when I get back. Another lie, although it is an emergency,
my life or death, but I can't say that. I'm hoping I can look at the
situation rationally when I'm out of town and out of danger, and
some idea will come to me, besides my murder or suicide. It seems
that suicide is the only thing in my control—I could "bounce," as
the skydivers say, fast and hard, no explanation, nobody to blame
but myself. I visualize tracking toward the airport, turning left and
right, zigzagging, finally plowing my own grave, so somebody can
just throw a few shovels of dirt on top. Tom will get over me in no
time. I hate knowing that.

In the morning, Tom leaves to get his rig and tie up some
details. I tell him I have to help Jerry tranquilize a couple of rhinos
and administer their TB tests, but I should be able to leave by two,
at the latest. I can go straight from the park to Tom's. I pack quickly
and tell Corey what calls to make. She's happy to have a couple
days off, except for stopping by to feed and walk the boarders and
the kids—they're a lot less trouble than her real kids. We're going
to take my car, rather than leave it around where something might
happen.

Gerald and I have just finished darting the last rhino and I'm in the truck, wiping my face, when Tom calls on the cell phone. "How's it going?

"Fine. I just have to take the stuff back to the office and then I'll be ready to head out."

"I'm hoping we can get there in time to put up our tent before dinner."

"Shouldn't be a problem."

"Also, I need you to bring your bag. I've got a big cub that came in with a sore paw. He might need to be knocked out to treat."

I can't imagine he's got one that large, but I have everything I need in my bag. Tom says to hurry so I'll have time for Biggun, as he calls the cub. I drive straight from the field to my car and pass the office without stopping. I've already filled Nibblefoot's feeder with rat pellets and freshened her water bottle. She'll be okay for a week.

When I get to his place, Tom comes out and walks me directly back to the cub. I want to fold into his arms, but I walk fast beside him, wanting to get the whole thing over and get out of there. We walk to the cage, and I can't believe the size of him, probably ninety pounds, nine or ten months old. He's sleeping on his back like a kitten, and I tell Tom that I want to try to handle him without tranquilizing. We go in quietly and Tom points out the right front paw. I bend and take a close look without touching. I can't see a thing.

"Be ready to pin him while I pick up the foot," I tell him.

His eyes get big, and he takes a ready position. I gently pick up the paw. The lion opens his eyes and looks at me, but Tom is stroking his ears and he doesn't try to lunge—good-natured. I poke around between the pads, expecting a reaction, but the lion just lifts his head and watches.

"He's a sweetheart," Tom says.

"Don't count on it." I move the joint back and forth at the

ankle. "That's a good boy, Biggun." Not a flinch. "I can't find any-thing," I tell Tom. "Let's go out and see how he walks. It could be a strained muscle."

Tom gets to his feet and we step away. The lion pulls himself up, lazylike, stretches, and stands looking at us. "Let's go out and give him some room."

We stand outside the cage and watch. He goes to the water bowl. "He's walking fine. I can't see a problem."

"Maybe he had a burr or something and got it out."

"Possible. Whatever it was, it's okay now."

"Then let's hit the road," Tom says. "Yahoo—time to skydive!"

"Who's going to take care of him?"

"My partner will stop over—the old keeper. He'll let me know if there's a problem. He's got the DZ number up there."

I tell Tom we're going to have to vaccinate the lion as soon as we get back. "Who the hell is going to take a cub this size?" I ask him.

"Big guy. Scared of nothin'."

"I don't get it. I just can't understand what these people are thinking."

"He doesn't have to think. He's got enough money to hire somebody to do his thinking for him."

"Sounds like he hasn't filled the position."

Tom shrugs it off. "I don't know anything and I don't dwell on it. I just deliver. There's a lot worse stuff happening to human beings in this world—instead of animals—to worry about."

It's meant to sting, and there's nothing I can say. He knows my position, and he knows I'll keep doing the checkups, for fear the animals won't get care otherwise, and because he knows I'll do almost anything he says.

I'm not happy, but I put it out of my mind. I'm forgetting all my worries for the week. I put my medical bag on the seat and Tom runs in to get his rig and bag of clothes.

By noon, we're on Route 27, headed north, and I feel the sunshine and blue sky evaporating the guilt and fear of the day and the weeks before that. I'm a new person. All I can think about is getting out of a plane, soaring, survival on my own terms. The world of other people's control has faded away with the last row of sugarcane.

I reach and take Tom's hand. He's loose and relaxed, and he turns to me with a smile that drives me into the seat. It's his special power, a force as strong as gravity that squeezes my chest with a rush of exhilaration. His effect on me is a fucking law of nature. "Sweetheart," he says, and puts his hand on my thigh, "you have no idea how much fun we're going to have."

His words make me wet instantly. "I have some idea," I say. "I have a pretty good idea."

We turn west on US 60, and the scent of orange blossoms fills the truck with warm perfume. It's a short drive from there to the drop zone—a week of freedom.

Tom has brought a tent and sleeping bags, and we set up in the small grassy camping area across from the hangar. Then we walk through the huge open structure, past the packing and dirt diving, swarms of people in colorful jumpsuits. The landing area spreads out on both open sides of the hangar, one field parallel and one perpendicular. I realize that you can choose where to land according to the wind direction, but there's a lot of space on either side, the line of trees way beyond. Blue meets the green, not a cloud in the sky, a steady breeze. Perfect conditions.

DZ Mom and Jacques are parked, motor home and kitchen, beside the hangar, so they have a perfect view of inside and out. People are seated at wooden spool tables, eating. Luisa goes by on her bicycle and stops to give me a hug. I feel her warmth from the soft skin of her cheek pressed against mine and relax even more— these people are now my friends. "Marcia's here, too, and Mickey and Lizz, Libby, Dido, Chris, Mario—more coming tonight. Brian's here—nice guy from Chicago." She throws out the names like we're all old friends, and I know we will be before the week's over.

DZ Mom yells through the kitchen screen. "Hey, y'all—bastard son and bastard daughter. Get your asses in here and say hi to your mother."

She opens the door. Her hair is spiked in orange and blond. Her hands are on her hips. "You kids better get in here and give me a hug—I'll send your bastard daddy out there to whip your asses!"

We both laugh. Tom puts his hand on the back of my neck and we walk the few yards and up the steps into the shining aluminum cabooselike structure. It seems strange having it in a different place.

DZ Mom wraps her arms around me and I smell a roast cooking in the oven, visualize carrots, onions, and potatoes simmering in the juice. I'm in heaven. This is a home like I never had, having grown up on hummus and raw veggies eaten from the fridge. All I have to do is relax and enjoy—the food, the people, the sport, all in one package, with the most beautiful man alive. I don't know how I lived to deserve all this. If I die at the end of the week, all the hard work and deprivation of my life will be equaled by the happiness— maybe the answer to life and death. Achieve balance and the job is done. Follow Grandma into the light and start all over. Doesn't sound so bad. A quote I've seen on a skydiving poster comes to mind: "Death is just another horizon beyond which we cannot see."

"Hey, Des, don't look so serious."

DZ Mom is wide-eyed, hands on hips, making fun of me, and I notice how blue her eyes are, not piercing like Tom's, but bright, open, and innocent.

We spend a few minutes talking about how good we have it, perfect weather, days of fun ahead. Tom says we ought to manifest for a jump, get me a rental rig. We head out to get started, and in thirty minutes, we board the Casa. It's luxury compared to sitting on the floor of the Porter with your knees and legs pinned by the person in front of you, sometimes your ass on a seat belt coupling. I hold a tight smile and try to ignore the shifting gas in my abdomen. My helmet and goggles are clutched on my lap to keep my fingers from shaking. The tension seems to build with each sky-dive. I'm told that I'll feel better around number sixty—a number I can't imagine I'll ever reach.

I watch the ground drop away beyond the open rear door. It's a wide view of trees and ponds. "Nice view, huh?" Tom yells above the engine. "You can chuck out ten or twelve people at a time."

I nod. "I hope I can find the airport," I yell back.

"You will. Don't worry. Follow me." He pats my hand. "We'll get you in on a couple of three-ways before the week's out. I want to try to do a horny gorilla with you, too." He gives me a sexy grin.

I don't know about any of that. I nod again and figure I'll ask for details later. I've seen videos—everyone having so much fun—a mass of arms and legs heaving out of the plane—fearless, unlike me.

When the red light comes on, Tom motions me to stand up. We're last out because I'm going to pull higher than the rest, but he wants to give my gear one more check. I'm thinking about the sabotage of my last jump. It's nothing he could have seen in a routine inspection.

He motions me around and checks my reserve pin. He takes my shoulders and turns me back. "You're fine!" he yells. "Take it easy. You'll do great." He tilts my head up for a kiss and then it's time to move.

I take a breath and consciously throw off all thinking. Every possible precaution has been taken. Be cool and live.

I adjust my goggles and take a deep breath, letting the air back out slowly. We wait while the groups in front of us go out. Tom looks around the plane and puts his hand on my shoulder. I look at

his lips, expecting to read one last word of caution or encouragement. He puts his mouth near my ear. "Fuck. I have to tell you this
so you know. Swan's coming here for the boogie. I just found out."

A knife goes through me. I look to see who's sitting next to
him, who could have told him on the plane. Nobody around I recognize. "She's skydiving?" I yell back.

"Yeah, she got me into it, then quit. Now she's started up
again."

This is news I don't need, for Christ's sake. I lurch with the
slight movement of the plane as the group in front of us goes out.

I can't think. I want to bury my face in my hands and scream,
but we're on the edge of the plane in one blurred movement. Tom
stands with his back to the door and I'm in front of him. I know he
can see my burning eyes inside my goggles. He takes my shoulder
grips, and I grab his in return. He counts—ready, set, go—we're
out. I feel the air come up under me and start to raise me above
Tom. I arch as hard as I can in response and feel him push me
down. Soon we're flying flat and stable. He smiles and moves in for
a kiss, trying to make up for his announcement. He keeps kissing
until I turn my head to break him off and glance at my wrist—
we're only down to ten thousand feet.

We've planned for me to fly all the way around him, taking
grips on each leg and back to the beginning. I start to the right, but
slip away. I'm thirty feet off before I know it. I stick my legs out and
start moving forward slowly, afraid I'll get up too much speed and
collide. He flies to me and takes my left hand. I give him my right.
He nods, and I know he's ready to let me go. I feel the release and
slide away again. Feet out—my thinking is too late. This time
when he takes my wrists, I shake my head no. I can't do it. The
altimeter shows six thousand feet. I don't have the energy to try it
again.

He pulls me close for another kiss. This one is brief. I glance at
my altimeter—4,500 feet. I break from his fingers, turn, and go,

knowing he'll track in the opposite direction. I pull and feel the relief of a perfect opening.

I'm shaky under canopy, not sure of anything, but I spot the airport straight ahead. I choose the south side of the hangar, and circle there, far from telephone poles and barbed-wire fences. I skid in my landing, tearing up the dry grass, landing on my ass, but it doesn't hurt. The exhilaration hits me as I stand and begin to ball the nylon into a mass I can carry. Tom must be inside the hangar already. His small canopy is much faster than the huge one I'm using.

I start walking, feeling good, until the other thought returns— "Swan." I realize I've said her name out loud. She's coming here— what does that mean? Christ. She's probably an expert skydiver. Why in the world didn't Tom tell me that she might come around? Why tell me then, in the plane? Is there anything she doesn't do? I feel my throat tightening up.

I put on a partial smile to walk into the hangar. I scan the crowd in jumpsuits, looking at the women and expecting to see Swan glowing in creamy white. I drop my rental rig in a pile for the packer, go over to my bag by the couch, and strip off my jumpsuit. I still don't see Tom. I walk on back toward DZ Mom's. Finally, he comes from around the kitchen, carrying a beer. "Last load's down," he says. "Beer light is on." I reach for the beer without a word and take a big gulp. He puts his arm around me and tilts his forehead against mine. "What are we gonna do?" he whispers. I feel his warm breath.

"Don't ask me. I have no idea."

"Got to pack up my rig," he says. "Sit down with DZ Mom and take it easy. We'll talk later."

I go inside the kitchen and take a stool. "Want me to fix you a plate?" DZ Mom asks.

I nod. I know she's reading something in my face or she would've told me to fix my own plate. We're not close enough for her to ask. I wonder how close she is with Swan. "Thanks," I say, "I'm beat."

I'm not hungry, but it's easier to eat than talk. I'm just finishing when Tom comes in. He eats and trades silliness with Mom while I sit and try to smile. She looks at us with concern. Afterward, Tom and I walk into the darkness. A night fog has rolled over the field and spread the glow from the lights. We keep going until we're far enough that nobody can hear. Everyone is in silhouette by the campfire. We sit on the edge of the runway and Tom spots a shooting star. I'm numb to his enthusiasm. The field is unearthly, like the DZ at Clewiston, enormous, haunting space, still not big enough. The smell of orange blossoms that was so fresh and clean when we arrived has thickened and hangs in my nostrils. I can't think of anything to say.

"We have to do something," Tom says. "She's on you like a—"

"I know. I know."

"I can't remember the last time she came to a boogie."

"She's an expert, right?"

Tom nods. "Couple thousands jumps—she's spent a lot of time in the wind tunnel lately, practicing."

"We have to leave," I tell him.

He takes my hand and squeezes it. "There's nowhere to go. It's time to do something."

I shake my head.

"You have what you need in your bag."

"What are you talking about?"

"That tranquilizer you were using on the rhinos, the M-ninety-nine. Didn't you say the slightest residue was lethal for humans?"

"Yes, I have that, but—"

I lower my eyes to the runway and feel my own breathing. My face and throat are tight.

"I've been thinking about this," he says. "With Swan's heart problem, they'll think it's natural. Her family will make sure there's no autopsy. I remember when her aunt died. They didn't want anybody 'defiling' her body, so they got their family doctor to sign the death certificate."

"Don't tell me this." I'm cold with fear. I see he's put some thought into it. "A heart condition? You never said anything about that."

He shrugs. "Found out after she'd been skydiving for a year, but she wouldn't quit. She said she would have died of the stress during AFF if it was gonna kill her—that skydiving kept her alive."

I can't believe it. "Are you sure? What kind of heart condition?"

"An SVT—whatever that is. She never would talk about it—in denial, I guess. It's the only problem she ever had that couldn't be fixed with money."

"Supraventricular tachycardia? She had an electrocardiogram?"

Tom moves close. "Yeah. One time after a jump, she couldn't get her breath; it was a close call. That's why she stopped for a while."

"So you think I can just prick her with M-ninety-nine and stop her breathing? Get away with that? No way—it's insane."

He strokes my arm. "I'm telling you, there'd be no suspicion of murder. It takes so little of the stuff and she's gone. They're not gonna test for any weird substances like M-ninety-nine when it's heart failure, like her doctor's been expecting—caused by skydiving stress."

"It would be likely they'd miss it, but the fact that people know we're together—"

"I'd be the suspect—the ex. I'm the obvious one."

"I don't want you getting the electric chair, either."

"Don't worry about me. I'll make sure I have an alibi. People have seen some of our argument, my bad behavior, but they know how long we've been apart. Nobody's going to think a thing about murder. It'll just be natural, baby. You can do it."

"No, I can't," I whisper. "It won't be natural. It's murder."

"Self-defense, baby. Listen, sweetie, she'll be staying at the Chalet Suzanne, the only place good enough for a princess in Lake Wales. She always gets the same room. They have a runway, so she flies in on her private plane."

I feel myself shaking. I'm thinking that I could administer the necessary amount without the site being perceptible. Or plead self-defense. No.

"Everything the best for Swan."

"You knew all along she was going to be here."

"No, I didn't. I thought you and me were going to have a nice week together. She's been too busy with the horses and hasn't sky-dived in a year—actually, that's a perfect reason for extra stress on her heart."

"It's just a coincidence you asked me to bring my bag to treat the cub?"

"You saw his size. I did remember what you told me about the kinds of tranquilizers—but not for this weekend. It's convenient you brought the stuff along—fate—like we're meant to do it."

"*We* are? Or *I* am?"

"Us. You and me. Betty—the owner—told me Swan ordered a new canopy sent here to be put into her container. She'll be coming in day after tomorrow to pick it up and spend the rest of the week jumping."

I can't say anything. It's so far-fetched to think I could go to her hotel room and . . .

"You know there's nothing else to do. She's got to be here for a purpose other than skydiving. You have to beat her to it."

"That's impossible. I can't break into her room."

"No problem."

"What?"

"I have the key."

My chest tightens. A sob catches in my throat and I can't speak.

"Listen. Calm down." He puts his arm close around my head and presses my face to his chest.

My body shudders because I know he planned this whole thing. He wants me to go over there and kill her. I can't move, can't think. Tom holds me. I press myself closer, until his stillness and warmth take over my body.

"Look, she's not even here yet. I have a key from last year—never thought to take it off my key ring."

I look at him and frown. It's all too strange. He fishes into his pocket for the jangling chunk of keys he carries.

"Her room is Blue Skies West. She always reserves ahead, and I'm sure they never change the locks—antique doors. Not a lot of crime in that area."

"I just walk into her room and dart her, huh?" I'm beginning to get angry. "Why don't you do it? Since you're the one who doesn't want to go to the police, why don't you go over there and do it? I'll show you how to pull the trigger—it's easy."

I'm sarcastic, trying to make Tom feel the ridiculousness of it, but he pauses, considering. "I can't go over there. Most of the staff know me."

I shake my head and he pulls me to his shoulder again. I see how far this has come. I'm boxed in, desperate to end the nightmare of her and start living without fear, without her constricting everything we do, her sociopathic personality thriving on my panic. I know part of my feeling is envy, that she has so much wealth and power, especially the part of Tom she owns. I feel a taint she's put on his character, no doubt from using him so well, and then making it clear that he was never up to her classy standards, regardless of his body and how hard he might try.

Tom unhooks my arms from around him and smooths back my hair. "It'll be easy. She always wears earplugs—claims she needs 'em to sleep."

I cringe from his intimate knowledge of her, the reminder of them together in bed.

"It's only a few miles up the road. Just go over there and take a look. Nobody knows you. You can have lunch and wander around—it's a tourist attraction."

I open my mouth but can't answer. He's suggesting I case the place as a lunchtime diversion. Just like when he sent me to the stables.

"Look. You're a doctor. You have the authority to decide on life or death, and you do it with confidence when it comes to animals." He takes my shoulders. "There's no difference. Somebody has to end this—and I don't want it to be her."

"I know."

"All right. Give me the stuff. I'll do it. It's more of a risk for me, but I'm willing to take it, if I have to—for you."

I see the white-hot steel in his eyes. "No. You couldn't. I'd have to—to make it look right."

"Just go and check out the place. Then you can tell me what you want to do."

I nod and wipe my eyes, stand on tiptoe to take a kiss. Tom folds me inside his arms and I feel his solid strength and wonder how Swan could do anything besides love him.

"Let's go be sociable at the fire," he says. He points to the starry sky. "We've already been given our luck for the night."

"What luck?"

"The shooting star."

"I didn't see it."

"Doesn't matter. You're with me—remember that, sweetheart. I got enough luck for both of us."

He takes my hand and we walk over to the fire. There are ten people or so on stumps around it, laughing, DZ Mom and Jacques, Marcia, Luisa, and Steve among them. A couple guys are talking together in German.

We stand close. My clothes are cold and damp.

"Great fire," Tom says. He turns to me. "Frenchy chops wood and builds the fire every day. This place is filled with characters. He's close to eighty and still makes the first load every morning. He figures if he lives through it, he'll have a good day. He's jumped all over the world for years and years—lots of good days."

"Uh-huh."

"Yeah," Jacques says. "We have to burn up all these boxes or he won't make a fire for us tomorrow." He takes a box from the pile of empty beer cases and sets it on top of the burning logs.

The box catches quickly and Tom moves me back as it flares up. "Scorch your legs," he says.

I'm barely conscious of the surroundings, with all that's on my mind. In a minute, Tom pulls me by the hand and we say our good nights. I think, At least he's not trying to pretend we're not together anymore.

He holds open the flap and I throw myself in onto the soft sleeping bag and air mattress. Tom piles right in on top of me. "Not a soul nearby," he says. He wraps me up in his arms, taking my hair in his hands, his mouth to my neck. His hand moves down into my sweatpants. His fingers are still warm from the fire. I never would've thought it could work, but I stop thinking and feel the gush of juices he brings so easily.

I PUT ON A CRISP WHITE DRESS IN the morning and drive over to Chalet Suzanne. I can rationalize a visit to one of the most famous restaurants in the state. North on 27, a right turn after the Eagle Ridge Mall. With the giant billboard they've got out, I have no trouble finding the street. Chalet Suzanne Road winds through an orange grove, such a peaceful setting, another place tainted by the life I'm living inside myself.

I turn onto Chalet Suzanne Lane, a narrow brick road, and begin to feel overwhelmed by quaintness as I glimpse the small pseudo-European village on the edge of a hill overlooking a lake. A feeling of sickness comes over me. I know it's connected with Swan and probably has nothing to do with the actual place. But there's something too much, too rich, in the Easter egg–pastel architecture. It's a miniature railroad landscape, a place where Hercule Poirot or Miss Marple would have felt right at home, a place begging for murder. I pass a stand of trees and on my left are horses. Horses. Swan can ride and skydive and luxuriate in the pool and her quaint room, where maybe she would invite Tom for a tryst, if she felt in the mood for his smooth body. One of the horses is a white Arabian, with a dish face and the typical swanlike curve of the neck—for her, of course. It's a taller, sturdier horse than her pasofino, less of a strutter, with a magnificent plume for a tail. Its coat shines in the sun and it turns toward me with a whip of its mane. Maybe it's not hers, but the coincidence is too much. I know it's hers, just like the rest. She can afford to keep a horse wherever she goes. I picture her perky face and sharp clip across the stable. Now I can hate her for all of it.

I pass an elaborate fountain, maybe fifty feet in diameter, nymphs and stalks of cattails amid an arched spray. The scene before me is peaked roofs, gingerbread, and stained glass, patterned gardens of geraniums, snapdragons, and petunias, tender blossoms that can't survive the hot Florida sun for long. They must be newly planted. I park in front of the restaurant and walk down the rough brick to the entrance.

I step into a forest of antique furniture of all eras and nations. There's an overall Eastern feel, with giant jars and brass statues mingled among dark wood tables and uncomfortably delicate sofas on the edges of heavy Oriental rugs. Nothing is real, including the errand I'm here on. I keep walking past the dim bar on the right and follow the unmistakable path through the furniture toward the eating area. I'm living a dark fantasy. An evil Alice in Wonderland spirit pushes me on.

It's not quite noon, and there's nobody around. I pick up the menu—forty-six dollars for lobster Newburg for lunch. I haven't spent that in a month of lunches in Pahokee. I knew this place couldn't be for real. I scan further—chicken salad, thirty-one dollars. That's almost the price of two skydives. I don't know if I'll eat. I take a postcard of the rooms and stand before wooden shelves of canned soup—mushroom seafood bisque, watercress, moon soup, whatever that is.

"Would you like a table?"

"No. I'm . . . just looking around a little."

She nods and goes through a door to the kitchen. I hear her answering someone. "No. She's just a looker," she says.

That's good. They're used to "lookers." I can't really afford a thirty-dollar lunch now that I'm taking off work and skydiving. I guess it never occurred to Tom. He's used to a woman with money.

I turn and head back out. My stomach is queasy.

I turn to the little village of rooms, pass the pool. They're all different styles and heights, in two parallel lines on the hill above the lake. If I wasn't feeling so much dread, I could appreciate the landscaping and hills in Florida. I walk down the middle, looking for Blue Skies West. Each room has its name above the door. It's as quaint as I can imagine. The door of Orchid is open, and I pause to look at the carved antiques and perfect mixture of flowered and checked fabrics, ruffles and lace. It's a dream world—or a nightmare.

I come to the tallest building, a blue two-story with a turret, windows all around. BLUE SKIES WEST it says above the door. I don't dare go up the steps. I'll have to do that in the dark. I try to imprint the setup on my memory, so I won't stumble or make a noise. I don't know how I'm going to do this. I shudder, realizing I'm making a plan.

I finish the walk to the end, like a tourist would do, killing time on the outside, eating myself alive inside. I pass one of the maids in her uniform, say good morning and smile, pretending my stomach isn't ready to leap from my throat.

Once I start walking toward my car, I have to hold myself back. I want to run and fly from this lovely piece of civilization, gardens sprinkled with sunshine, all poisoned by my evil intentions. I watch my shadow on the uneven brick as I control my steps. It must be done. It must be done. I realize I'm walking to a rhythm, touching a foot to a brick with each word. It must be done. I don't know how I got here, to this place in my mind. She could die in much worse ways. It will be an easy death, no fear, no pain. She's had everything she's ever wanted except to see me dead, and she won't get that.

I come out of Chalet Suzanne Lane and turn onto the main road. In a few minutes, I realize I've gone in the wrong direction. The pressure is kicking in. I go a little farther, looking for a place to turn around. I see a sign: SPOOK HILL. It says to put the car in neutral and let it roll. I'm right there on the hill by myself, so I put my foot on the clutch, shift, take my foot slightly off the brake. I expect nothing, a silly joke, but as the car begins to roll, I feel it. I would swear I'm moving forward. It's an uncomfortable feeling. Like I don't know what's real. My perception is reversed. I shift back into first and hit the gas. Already I've rolled halfway down. I make the crest, pull off the road, turn around quickly. I don't know why I tried to scare myself worse. I want to get back to the drop zone, where I can put everything out of my mind until the time comes. A jump is the only thing that will work. If I die, I won't have to finish the plan.

When I get back, I sign right up for a jump, not even looking for Tom. I'll jump by myself and practice my tracking. I need to fly alone. I rent a rig—no computer, but I don't care. I can die only once. Once I've gotten my jumpsuit on, it's time to go outside and line up. The Casa ride seems short, and my guts barely have time to cramp. I'm calmer than usual, maybe because death would be a relief. I'm last out, and when my turn comes, I run all the way from the front of the plane and fling myself out the back, drop as if on a feather bed, flat, head up, as Tom has told me. The wind below the plane flings my legs above my head, but they settle back flat. I'm free and the sky is in my control.

I look around at the small lakes and spread of fields below. The world is mine to keep or give up. It's lovely and peaceful, despite the roar of wind and the force of it against my body. I make a couple of slow turns, taking in the beauty, feeling the air. I look at the altimeter as I'm passing seven thousand feet, look around some more . . . six thousand. I track perpendicular to the plane, stop, but I don't pull. I have a few more seconds . . . four thousand—needle zooming—3,500 . . . How fast it goes. I could die doing nothing. Two thousand . . . 1,500 . . . My hand goes down by itself and flings the pilot chute. It yanks out the main. I watch it undulate above me, puff, spring wide open. "It's there and it's square," I say to nobody. I take a huge breath of sky.

Fate didn't want me. If I'd had a problem, there would have been no time to cut away and pull the reserve. I grab the toggles and give them a tug. I'm already at 750 feet—sure to get a tough lecture if anybody saw or finds out how low I pulled. As a novice, I might get banned from the drop zone. The landing area? On my right. I just need to head downwind a short distance and turn into my landing leg. The wind is strong, and I'm there in seconds. I make one of my smoothest landings ever, flaring perfectly, lightly touching down, feeling the ecstasy of living, despite what it might bring. Suicide, I see, is not an option.

That night after dinner, Tom walks me out on the runway again. He tells me that Swan has arrived and that she called Betty to make sure everything was set for the morning. I ask how he knows all this, and he says that Betty is "so easy to talk to." He asked questions, acting concerned and she reassured him. He told her it'd been a rough breakup and that he doesn't want Swan to know he still cares.

He says Swan likes to get an early start and jump back to back all day, with only a break for lunch. She's always trying new rigs, which she alternates with her favorite, the one she's bought the new canopy for.

He sits, takes my hand, and pulls me down next to him on the edge of the runway, strokes his fingers along my arm. "Chalet Suzanne is a quiet place, a lot of old people. You can get there around three and not see a soul."

My throat tightens and my hands turn to ice.

"I could drive you and stay in the car, if you want, but I was thinking I should wait here. Just in case somebody comes by—it would look funny if they couldn't find us. This way, I can always say you're asleep in the tent."

"The car will be gone."

"No problem. That's why I parked across the street—so nobody will notice."

We stay up late around the fire, until the last few partyers, some young pilots, have stumbled off. It's almost two. I quietly sip the cup of diet Pepsi I've been carrying around all night, pretending to have a good old time slugging down rum and Coke. It's a relief when everybody's gone and I can settle into the cold rock-hardness I feel.

"Let's go over to the tent," Tom says. "You should put on a white shirt and dark pants. That way, if anybody sees you, you'll look like staff."

"I didn't bring a white shirt."

"I have one that'll work."

I look at him in pure terror.

"Just get in there, stick her, and get out. She sleeps like a log in her earplugs. Don't worry."

"It's goddamned murder."

"That's good." He pats my shoulder. "You can say the word. That's what somebody who doesn't know what's been going on would call it. But you and me know it's self-defense. You can't go by the law on this. You have to trust me." He takes my face in his hands and kisses my mouth softly, moving all around my lips. "You're the only one who can save yourself. You have the means and the guts to do it. You have to make the decision about who's going to live."

I nod, knowing he's right. The situation can't go on. It's like putting a rabid animal to sleep, necessary and painless. I dress, tucking his shirt into my jeans. "It's not much of a fucking plan."

"It's simple. That's the best." He hands me a light rain jacket. "You never know when it might rain," he says.

"Tonight?"

"You need the pockets."

"Right." I sigh.

He puts his arms around me for a tight hug of encouragement, as if I'm going to do my duty in some humanitarian effort, instead of playing God. Okay. She's hateful and she wants to kill me. As I stoop and raise my shoulders out of the tent, he pats my ass. It makes me shudder.

The car feels unfamiliar as I get in. The mist has settled. Bug guts and moisture coat the window. I take the syringe from my bag, carefully open the specially sealed vial, and touch the tip of the needle into the liquid M-99. I cap it and put it in my pocket, then grab some surgical gloves and my penlight. I find the ignition and pull out, barely able to see, but not wanting to sit there and make noise. I pump the windshield spray as I stop to make the turn on Highway 60, and the bug smear turns to a thin cream that makes every light a glare. I'm sweating despite the chills inside me.

As I pull into Chalet Suzanne Road, I think of Spook Hill up ahead, the trick of perception, the inadequate human brain. Human evil. Her evil. The orange trees are ghosted with mist and nothing seems real. I feel like I'm playing my part in a movie by Alfred Hitchcock. It will soon be over.

I park among the cars in the lot and walk toward the foggy village. It's deadly quiet, and I try not to scrape with my footsteps. I cut through to the little interior path, and it's there—Blue Skies West—in all of its cheesy, fake quaintness. I wonder if Swan originally took this room thinking of Tom's eyes, rather than skydiving. I hate her.

I hold my breath and start up the stairs, easing my weight on the side of each step, where it's less likely to creak—something I read years ago, never dreaming I'd use it.

I listen outside the door. No noise, no light. Even if she's wearing earplugs, I'm not taking any chances. I reach into my pocket for the syringe.

I glance down at the walkway to be sure I'm still alone. I take the syringe from my pocket, leaving it capped. I slip the key into the lock with the other hand. If it makes a click, I'll just run, forget the whole thing. The key goes in and I turn the knob slowly. The click is so faint that I barely hear it. I stand listening. No sound. I remember the gloves in my pocket. I don't have enough hands, so I have to put the syringe back while I stretch on the glove. One will do. My hands are clammy and it takes time to work each finger into the tight latex. I'm sweating in my own heat, a hothouse inside the waterproof jacket. Finally, the glove's on well enough. I reach down and rub the doorknob on the side where I've touched it to get rid of the fingerprints—not that I expect anyone to investigate.

I take out the syringe again, uncap it this time, dropping the cap into my pocket, and push the door open a couple of inches. I can't see anything inside, just black. Cold air conditioning hits my face. I don't want to stand there too long. I look behind me down the walk. I turn back, and with one finger, I push the door a centimeter at a time, ready to stop if there's the slightest creak. Soon I can see the lower part of the bed by the light from the turret windows. She's under the covers, her face in shadow, one arm folded on top. I steady myself.

I continue pushing slowly, my eyes riveted on her hand, my target. I can grab her hand, push the covers over her face, and throw my weight on top of her head and arms for the second it will take to slip the needle under a nail. With all the practice I've had on struggling animals, I know I can do it in one try. I have the advantage of surprise. Her sounds will be muffled by the quilt and my body as she takes those last strangled breaths. I won't have to look at her face as she dies.

I step inside, leaving the door as it is, thinking it's less risky. I take out my penlight. I put it in my mouth, ridiculously, like I've seen in the movies, so I have a free hand. I take one small step, another, another. I glance at her head above the sheet, but it's too dark to see her clearly. I focus the penlight, steady my hand, and bring up the syringe, taking the last steps. I stumble. I grab the brass bedpost to catch myself. It's solid and holds steady, but I'm scared to death—the soft scuff of my shoe, a slight vibration of the bed . . . I'm shaking. I stare hard at her head on the pillow, keeping low, hiding the penlight in my palm. I realize that she's still sleeping—but it's not her. I'm sure it's not her. The hair is dark, very dark, and long. It's spread across the pillow, falling into the ruffles at the edge of the pillowcase. I strain to focus more clearly. It's the older woman—the stable help. Why is she sleeping in Swan's bed?

I switch off the penlight and uncrouch slowly. There's no other bed, nobody else here. All I want to do is get out. I see that I tripped on the leg strap of a rig resting against the base of a chair. There's not much space between all the overstuffed furniture, and the room is filled with suitcases and skydiving gear.

My brain starts to function: This is Swan. I wrongly assumed that Swan was the blonde with the attitude. Didn't I mention her blond looks to Tom? He didn't correct me. I look at her sleeping. This is not the woman I came to kill, the greedy, spoiled, rich bitch I've created in my mind, an image made of hate and envy. I remember our short conversation, her courtesy. I visualize her paint-splattered shirt, the baggy jeans with sawdust on the knees. There was a feeling of kinship I can't ignore, regardless of her money—beyond the fact that we're women in love with the same man.

I find the cap in my pocket and slowly put it back on the needle, then drop the penlight back into my pocket, and begin my careful tiptoe to the door. I'm relieved, but I can't let the feeling take me. I step around the leg strap. The floor creaks. I freeze. I don't dare turn my face to look at the bed. A click—the room bursts into painful brilliance. Gold sparks fly. I can't see enough to make a rush for the door.

"Who are you?" Her words are loud, more fearful than threatening. I expect some guard will come running.

I'm frozen, trying to think why she hasn't recognized me after all her surveillance. She has no weapon. She rubs her eyes and removes her earplugs. She stares at me. Her voice is soft, incredulous, "Why are you in my room?"

It's the same tone that drew me to her in the stables, far from the knife edge of a heartless snob. She's regained her composure, and we're woman to woman. I have the need to tell it all, but I can't speak. I can't even believe it myself. I'm grasping for words that don't come.

"I don't carry much cash." She shakes her head. "You don't look like a thief."

"No. I'm not. It's a mistake—wrong room. Sorry."

She frowns. "Which one did you want? You look familiar."

"I don't know. I'm looking for someone—I'm sorry."

"How did you get in?"

"A key. Somehow . . ." I don't want to stand there until she figures it out. I can't come up with anything. I can't betray Tom. "The key—it fit."

She's still under the covers, not ready to stop me. She seems totally innocent of the evil intention I came with.

"I'm sorry," I say again. I glance at the open door and turn to make my break. My feet clomp loudly on the wood floor, but I hit the partially open door at a run. There's not a sound from Swan. I slam the door behind me and run down the stairs, my legs moving so fast, it's like a film in fast motion. I take the path and keep on running. No one in sight. If I'm lucky, she'll think I'm crazy, go back to sleep without calling the police. Nothing I can do but make sure she never sees me again.

I make it to the car without slowing down and start up the engine, my eyes trying to penetrate the mist. No one there.

On the way back to the drop zone, fear sweeps over me. I don't want to tell Tom what happened, that the whole thing is wrong. It's like I let him down. It all seems impossible now, going there with the intention to kill. I think of how close I came. Would I have done it? It's almost like it wasn't me—that person who broke into her room, daring to stand a few feet from her with a poised needle—tripping, grabbing the bedpost. The memory of the cold brass comes to mind. I wasn't wearing the glove on that hand. It's a good thing I didn't kill her—an understatement. I start to laugh, and it's clear that I'm hysterical, losing myself or getting myself back—I don't know which. I'm light-headed. All I want to do is get it over with—tell Tom, and get rid of the needle. I don't know what I'll do after that, but I can't kill her, as much as Tom might want me to, as much as I should hate her.

I park and get my bag and carefully take the needle out of the syringe. I stamp it through the layer of sod, deep into the sand. I don't have a thing in my head, but I feel relief. I walk back to the tent, ready for Tom's questions. I unzip the flap and climb inside.

He sits straight up. "Are you okay?"

I nod. He snatches me down onto the sleeping bag beside him. I nuzzle close and put my arm around his ribs, not wanting to say anything. He holds me and I feel my strength slipping away.

"You'll be fine. Now everything'll be okay. No more hiding and sneaking around for us; the danger is gone."

I grip him tighter. "I didn't do it."

"What? I can't hear you." He tilts my face up so I'm looking into those eyes. In the darkness, they're like animal eyes in the woods.

"I couldn't do it. She woke up."

His body goes stiff and his hand under my chin pushes my head back farther. "Fuck! Jesus Christ." He drops his hand. Ice comes into his voice. "Now what? What happened? Why didn't you do it?"

"I couldn't. I couldn't touch her. I ran. She didn't even know who I was."

"She didn't recognize you?"

"No. I don't understand that," I say.

"Neither do I. What the hell are we going to do? Jesus. Fuck. What the hell happened?"

"Why didn't you tell me she wasn't the blonde at the stable?"

"Didn't I? Must have been her half sister—what difference does it make?"

"A lot." I bite my lip hard to keep going. "I thought you said she was having me followed?"

"Yeah. You saw the car."

My head is filled with blackness. I can't get the smallest glint of understanding. I ask him again, "How come she didn't recognize me?"

"Fuck if I know."

"God. She will now. I had the syringe put away when she turned on the light, but she saw my face. I have to leave—now."

He shakes his head. "This is all fucked up. I don't know what to do. I can't leave without saying anything. Betty will wonder; she'll talk to Swan."

"I can't let her see me here."

He doesn't say anything. I keep waiting.

"It's a good thing I didn't do it. I nearly tripped—my fingerprints are all over the bedpost."

"You didn't wear the gloves?"

"Just the one." I put my arm behind him, pull myself tight to his body again, although he's stiff. "I'll leave before dawn. I'll wait in town."

"I guess I can hitch a ride. Fuck."

I rub his shoulder. "Do a couple jumps and then make up some excuse. I'll wait at the IHOP."

He lets out a long, slow exhale. "I don't know what's going to happen now—what somebody might say to Swan about you. Everybody knows we're here together. I never figured Swan'd still be alive."

"If she already knows everything about me, I don't see where this is any different. You're not making sense."

"She knows it all. Except that you're here. It's really fucked up, really, really fucked up."

"I'm leaving before she gets out of bed."

He turns on his side, away from me, and I realize that's the end of the conversation. I lie there, not attempting to touch him. I know he told me she knew everything about me and knew me on sight. I didn't make it up. That was the whole reason I went over there. I try to think back and straighten out exactly what he said, but my memory is vague. Why did he let me think she was the young blonde with the attitude? All the feelings of fear and hate are gone when I think about the real person I saw.

I curl up on my side of the sleeping bag. I'll be relieved to drive away in a couple hours, even though I don't know what I'll do then. There's a numbness inside me. I've been saved from making a hideous mistake, whatever happens.

I AWAKEN, AND IT'S STILL TOTAL darkness. Maybe only a few minutes have passed. Tom is sitting up.

"Let me have the car keys."

"What for?"

"Take it easy. I can't sleep. I'm gonna run down to the all-night grocery and get something to drink. Want anything?" His tone is cold.

"No thanks." I hand him my purse. "They're in there."

I wonder if that's where he's really going. He leaves and I stick my arm out of the tent to look at my watch: 4:05. I lie down but don't even try to sleep.

It's not too long till he comes back. I feel my body relax a little, pulse slowing. "What time is it?"

"Four-thirty or so."

That means he's been gone less than a half hour. Not long enough to get to Swan's room and back. I close my eyes but lie there awake. I feel Tom's arm go around me once, for a while, but I don't know if he's conscious of it.

At dawn, Tom is still sleeping, so I'm quiet as I change into my shorts. I don't want to talk about Swan or any plan. I get my stuff together and touch his arm. "I'm going."

"Huh?"

"Meet me at the IHOP, remember?"

He looks at me and wipes those eyes. "Yeah. Okay. I don't know what time. I wasn't counting on seeing Swan."

"I'll sit in the car while it's cool and go in for breakfast at nine. If you're not there in a reasonable time, I'll go into Wal-Mart. We passed it. Remember? Look for my car in the parking lot. Okay? I don't want to sit at IHOP too long."

"Yeah. I'll find you."

"Maybe you won't have to see Swan. Just get your rig."

"Yeah, maybe."

His eyes are hard to read at half-mast, but I don't really expect him to show up. I don't know what he'll do, but I feel separated from him already. I'm still in shock from my own actions. I kiss him on the cheek, without feeling, pick up my sack of clothes, and climb out of the tent. It's still misty, cool, and silent as I walk to the car. I step lightly. Even the light crunch of gravel is too real for the moment. I get to the car and try to stop my growing hysteria. I unlock the door, sling my bag to the passenger side, and scoot into the car. I grip the wheel. I can follow my own plan and drive normally into town for breakfast. I can do it. Soon I'm on Route 60. I turn south on 27.

I think of Spook Hill again—perceptions askew. Maybe it's Lake Wales or the entire state of Florida that alters the senses. There's a need for more warning signs along the road: WELCOME TO THE STATE OF FLORIDA. CAUTION: KEEP YOUR FOOT ON THE BRAKE AT ALL TIMES TO PREVENT BACKWARD MOVEMENT. CAUTION: YOUR EYES MIGHT BE CLOSED WHEN YOU THINK THEY ARE OPEN. CAUTION: YOU MIGHT BE AWAKE WHEN YOU BELIEVE YOU ARE DREAMING.

What will I do back in Pahokee? Disguise myself every time I venture out of the neighborhood? How much time before I can go grocery shopping without expecting Swan around the corner of every aisle? I can't kid myself. My face has been indelibly coded into her brain—and it wasn't before, not until I broke into her room to kill her.

IHOP isn't crowded, and I take a table for two by the window. I haven't eaten at one of these places since grad school. This is the first time I don't have a book open or that jittery feeling of having only minutes left to study for a test. I feel worse than that—never knew it was possible. If I had tears, they'd be dripping on my placemat. I don't expect Tom to show up, and I don't know why, yet I'm almost sure of it.

The waitress comes over with her poised pencil and I look down at the menu. "Silver dollar pancakes." I don't know if I can eat a single one.

"Coffee?"

"Please." I might sit here forever waiting for Tom, unable to move and make it all final.

The brown mug of coffee I remember so well is set in front of me and I tear open a pack of sugar. I can't keep from glancing outside, down the road, even though I don't know what kind of a vehicle Tom will be in. What if he can't get a ride? It wasn't a very good plan. What kind of excuse can he give for leaving? Maybe DZ Mom will be heading to town for supplies. He'll have to make up a good story.

The pancakes come. They look flat and dull. I remember when they were food for the gods, the assorted syrups gleaming like jewels in the fluorescent light. It was our treat when my roommate and I had "blood money"—spare bucks we got when we gave blood every sixty days or so.

I chew a few tasteless pancakes and sip my coffee. There's a newspaper in the next booth and I pick it up and start on the first section. I figure I can sit here for an hour or so reading, or trying to read. There's a death on the front page, a scuba-diving accident, a woman diving a wreck. The man last saw his wife following him to the surface, looking fine—then she was gone. Later, her body was found under the deck of the ship—investigation under way, insurance money involved. I'm thinking of how easy it would be to panic someone underwater. But if he planned to kill her, how could he act loving enough to get her go down with him in the first place?

I think of Tom trying to act normal with Swan. He can't let on that his girlfriend almost killed her—and that he helped set it up. It's a strange situation. He wants her dead.

It's 10:30, and I can't sit there anymore. I pay and go out to the car. It's already hot and uncomfortable. I drive the short distance to Wal-Mart and park under the row of trees at the end of the parking lot, the front seat in the shade. It's still hot. I recline the seat and shut my eyes. I don't have the composure to walk around the store. I go into a haze of grogginess and heat, a delirious swirling in my head.

Something touches my shoulder. I open my eyes.

"Can I have a ride, lady?"

I look up into his face. He's beautiful, his perfect tan skin gleaming with sweat. His mouth widens into a luscious, glorious smile. "Move over. I'll drive." A tremendous rush of relief flows through my whole body. He's turned my mind around again. "What time is it?"

He lifts my wrist and looks at my watch. "Noon—three after, to be exact." He opens the car door. "You're suffocating in there."

I step out and stretch, wipe sweat from my forehead. The tent and his gear bag are propped against the tire. He pulls my hair back and blows on my neck. I turn and give him a kiss. "You got out pretty fast."

"Real fast. I did the first load on the Casa and told Betty I pulled a hamstring. I limped around a little."

"You hitch a ride?"

"I told her you couldn't sleep in the tent and got a room at the Green Gables. DZ Mom gave me a ride over there on her way to the grocery. I took a cab here."

"The room would have been a better idea—I couldn't think."

"Oh well, we're ready to go now."

"Did you see Swan?"

"Nope. She wasn't there yet when I left."

"Great."

"We made a clean getaway. With a little luck, your name won't be connected."

"Just some mistaken loon in her bedroom. I hope she wasn't late from making a police report this morning."

"I doubt it. Not her style."

He gives me another hug and kiss and I walk over to the passenger side. I can't help thinking that Swan might not be the style Tom thinks.

"Been to Disney lately?" Tom asks.

"Disney? No. Why?"

"Less than an hour away. Wanna go?"

It's not anywhere I ever considered going—the epitome of phony commercialism, I'd always said—but since Tom mentioned it, I feel glee, like I'm in high school again.

DISNEY WORLD WITH THE HEAT

and fantasy makes me forget real life, almost. I'm back in Tom's arms on the rides, thinking there's nothing else I need. I'm safe. Life's normal—better than normal—if I don't think. We get home after midnight, go straight to bed, and zonk out. It feels good to be exhausted. We sleep close all night, and in the morning, it feels good to wake up in my own bed with Tom beside me, sun rays on his eyelashes. I hadn't expected him to stick by me.

I run my fingers delicately across Tom's forearm, feeling the silky hairs. His eyes open and he pulls me instantly into his arms. "Everything's going to be fine, beautiful." His face is dazzling in sleepiness, boyish blond hair falling over his eyes.

"You sure know how to wake up in the morning," I tell him. It's a clean slate between us. I can feel it.

"Always." He takes my hand under the sheet and places it on his solid, satin cock. He's harder than ever, and as he climbs on top, the smile never leaves his face. He looks me steadily in the eye, and I'm aware that he's laughing, chuckling to himself. I keep the rhythm going, letting the ecstasy flow down my back and through my hips. A sweat breaks out and I feel it running behind my thighs. A part of me is registering something about Tom's laugh, but the thought's not completely formed. I don't care. I let it go, let go. I come long and hard and lose momentum in sobs of pure wonder. Sexual concentration takes over Tom's face and he stops laughing.

I feel him climax and let go his long, low groan, as if every part of his being is forced inside me. I want to keep him there.

In a few minutes, the dogs start whining. I stumble through the apartment to let them out, then go back to lie down. Tom's arm comes across my waist. We fall back asleep in the luxury of having a morning when nobody knows we're here and no plans have to be made. We don't get up until eleven. I make some eggs and toast, then call and cancel Corey. I go to feed the boarded animals myself while Tom reads the paper and sips his coffee. It's a happy little family when I take my seat, with Angel and Clue snuffling around under the table, hoping for scraps. They trip us both when we take turns getting coffee. Tom chuckles as he reads.

After awhile, I need some conversation. "What's so funny?"

"Nothing—life." He hands me the movie section. "Anything good within a fifty-mile radius?" he asks.

"Sure. In Palm Beach." I'm happy to go to a movie with him, take my mind off life for another afternoon.

"Des."

"Here's *Shakespeare in Love,* the Academy Award winner." I glance up to see if he'll give it a chance.

He's not listening. His face is cold, eyes glazed. He points to an article halfway down the page. I can read the headline from across the table: SKYDIVER DIES IN LAKE WALES.

"Jesus, Tom. Who was it? Anybody we know?"

His eyes stay focused on the paper, lids flickering. I get up and go around to his side of the table.

The bile rises in my throat as I read the name Swan Rotherfield. I begin to choke. "Oh my God. Jesus Christ." I can't steady myself to read further.

Tom's voice is monotone. "Nothing out. The main had a bag lock and the reserve handle was still in place when they found her."

"Doesn't she have a computer?"

"No. She got rid of it—a friend was killed from a premature firing—entanglement. I don't use one, either."

"Why wouldn't she pull her reserve?"

"Who knows? Loss of altitude awareness? It happens. She had that heart problem, too, remember."

My stomach coils in a knot—the heart condition, the excuse.

Tom reads, " 'Jacques La Rose reported that she looked normal when they broke to track at four thousand feet.' "

My chest is tight. I don't know how to feel. "Fuck."

He tips his head toward me and those light blues are wide open and wild. "Your worries are over. What do you care?"

I stare back. His face is all wrong. "This is what you wanted."

"Only for you, sweetheart. Didn't you want it, too? To stop her from hurting you." He drops his eyes back to the newspaper.

I squat down on the floor to pet Angel. My feelings are a jumble of guilt, fear, and distrust. I want to think it's over, all by fate, but I can't. The feeling I've been trying to ignore since he met me in the parking lot is burning a hole in my guts.

I stand up on wobbly legs. "What time did it happen?"

"Let's see—they thought she'd landed out, so they didn't realize she was missing at first. Fuck. I left right away—that's why I didn't hear anything. It must have been the load after mine—eleven-thirty."

"How did you do it?"

He looks at me. "I didn't even jump with her."

"So what? You're a rigger. You could've done something before you left."

He scoots his chair out and pulls me into his lap, takes my hand. "Sweetheart? . . . You think I'm lying?"

My throat tightens. "It was self-defense, right? In advance—for me."

He looks at me, eyes wide and mouth open, that lock of hair falling into his eyes.

I've seen that face before, and I'm not buying it this time. "You better tell me the truth or I'll go to the police."

He sighs. "I doubt that."

I wait.

"You really don't want to hear this, but I guess I have to tell you."

"Tell me."

"I used the M-99."

I swallow. "M-99?"

"I darted her out the door with it."

"What?" I leap out of his lap. "You have the dart gun?"

He reaches to stroke my hair. "I did. It worked great. I darted her out the door and the dart fell right off. We were over the trees. That tiny thing—they'll never find it."

"Oh my God. Where's the gun?"

"I had to throw it away."

"Out the door?"

"I tracked over that little lake and let it go. I'm not connected, and neither are you." He takes my hand and squeezes it. "I didn't wanna be toting that gun around any more than necessary—just in case somebody was looking."

"You left before they found her?"

"Yeah. I shoved my canopy into my backpack and caught a ride."

"They're going to investigate. What if they find the M-99 in her system?"

"They won't. We talked this out, remember? No reason to test for anything unusual."

"How much was in the dart? It could kill anybody or anything out there."

"A touch, just like you said to use."

"I didn't say to use any of it!" I shake my head in despair. "Tell me the whole thing."

"I rerouted her bridle to give her the bag lock, in case the tranquilizer was slow. I didn't want her getting to the ground safely before it killed her. I figured if she just started choking, it would be enough. Anyway, it all worked perfectly."

"You packed her a container lock? Somebody must have seen you."

"I'm not a fool, baby. You should realize that by now. You know my sapphire-and-white rig?"

"Yeah. The one you usually use."

"Swan has one that looks exactly like it—from a team we were on. She outfitted the whole group, jumpsuits and all. Her rig was on the floor with a few others, as usual, so I just put mine down next to it. A few minutes later, I took hers over to the tent and fixed it, then brought it back. It took only a minute. Nobody noticed a thing. She was up on the Otter, so I knew she'd be using that rig for the next load, instead of repacking."

"She packed herself?"

"Mostly. She said it was good exercise. Nobody will know who packed her main from the last time. I just made a simple error."

"When did you prepare the dart gun?"

"In the morning, when I went out."

"Jesus Christ."

"After you fucked up, I had to do something. I never slept a wink all night thinking about it."

There's nothing more I can say. I might have killed her myself if I hadn't been so clumsy. Would I have? I can't answer. There's no self-righteousness left in me. He murdered because I failed. It's horrible.

"I timed it just right. She was in a group of eighteen, one of the last out—she's a good flier. She was a good flier. I knew it would work."

I'm looking at him, taking in the details he gives so calmly, feeling my fear intensify.

"I told them I wanted to be last out of the plane so I could open high, work with my canopy. I scooted down to the seat right beside her when her group was taking grips—I was in a perfect position. On "Go," I shot her on the left cheek, the plane side, where the pilots couldn't see. She probably thought I pinched her on the ass."

I'm wondering what her last thoughts must have been. "She didn't yell?"

"She was out the door too fast—flying."

"It must have taken a minute to affect her."

He shrugs. "She had time to fly her slot, because nobody reported anything. Perfect timing. I didn't know how the wind would change my aim if I shot her outside, so I couldn't take the chance. The dart fell off just as she hit the air. Perfect. Nobody could have seen it. With the mess when she bounced, they'll never find where I hit her. I counted to six and made my jump."

"What did she say on the way up? Anything about me?"

"Nope. She just glared at me."

I'm trying to imagine Swan glaring, but she wouldn't be very good at it, couldn't compete with Tom. Nobody can.

He says he's got a couple of errands to take care of and then he wants to make me dinner. His arms go around me and his cheek presses close. Then comes a sweet kiss that I barely return. He's trying to make things like they were. The warmth of being with him, cozy and secure, surrounds me—but it's mostly from memory, nothing to melt the icicle in my spine.

"I'll be home around five. I'll call you," he says.

"I'll be here. I'm not up to working today." I wonder how my words can come out so normally, like he hasn't become a killer and I haven't gone along with it.

He leaves, and I'm overwhelmed with the anxiety of being alone with my knowledge. I think of that gun somewhere in a lake, the empty dart stuck in a tree. My heart starts pumping. There's nothing I can do now. I push away the thought of turning us both in. The truth is clouded—no holes to spot through, no compass directions. I don't know if Swan needed to die. I don't know if she deserved it.

I can't stay at home. I decide to go to the drop zone and do a jump, hear all the talk, survive it, or give myself up. I want the fear of death. I want to feel those last seconds, like Swan did, to let fate have another chance at me.

THE DZ FEELS STRANGE WHEN I pull up. There are only a few cars. I've never been here when it wasn't jammed. I wonder if it's grief for Swan that's kept people away. I remember it's a weekday, normal. Nerves trigger my lower abdomen. I ignore the cramps and head right in to manifest for the next load. Lisa is at the desk.

"Hey," I say. "I decided to play hooky from work for once in my life." I hope she doesn't know me well enough to see behind the fake smile.

"Sounds good. Right now, there's nothing going up. Not enough people."

"Oh? I didn't think of that."

"I'll put you on the computer. There's a level one student who should be out of the classroom soon, ready to go. We can put you all up in the Cessna."

I wander into the hangar and sit down on the slumped piece of furniture—a typical DZ couch. Lee comes out of the loft where he does the repacks and starts to walk past, until he sees me. He puts up his finger to say wait and goes into the office, then comes back and hands me a piece of paper. "Roth asked me to give you this. He wanted your number, but I didn't know if I should give it out. I told him I'd give you his."

"Thanks." I shrug. A nervous twitch jerks my shoulder at the thought of Swan's brother.

"I told him you had an office but that I didn't have the number." He looks into my eyes. "Too bad about Swan, huh?"

"Yeah. Terrible."

"A lot of theories on what happened. Didn't make sense for her not to pull."

"I'm sure." I nod. "I never knew her."

"Oh. Yeah," he says. I can see he's thinking about my relationship with Tom.

Lee goes back to work, and I put Roth's number in my pocket. It can't be good for me to talk to him—the day after his sister's murder. It finally hits me about the loss to her family, the pain. I feel my chest caving in. It's all wrong.

I go to the pay phone and start to dial, then stop. Tom wouldn't want me to call Roth. I feel shaky, like my blood sugar is low, and I'm not thinking clearly. I go inside the manifest building and buy a bag of pretzels and a drink and sit next to Bear under the big tree. I don't know what to do. DZ Mom isn't around, since it's during the week. There's no one to talk to, even if I could. Not enough people to get the plane up. I put my arm across Bear's shoulder, close my eyes, and drift, wondering what Roth wants and if he's suspicious of me. I feel bad for him, but I don't know if I can get through a conversation. I can't answer any questions. I wonder how long before I get a call from the police.

I decide I owe Roth a call, before Tom hears that he's around asking questions. I might save a life.

There's nobody outside, so I go to the pay phone on the wall of manifest. Roth's voice mail answers and I'm struck dumb. I can't play it by ear and I'm not prepared. "Roth, this is Destiny Donne. Lee gave me your number. I don't know what to say. I'm sorry about your sister. Be careful." I give him my office number and tell him not to call at night.

I clunk the receiver three times on the cradle before I can manage to hang up. I shouldn't have said "Be careful." I walk back to the tree and drop down hard into the grass. I don't know what will happen now. I've put something into action. Roth might send the police right over for me and Tom.

I close my eyes and lean against the rough trunk. Bear has moved away. A wave of fatigue rolls over me. It's cool in the shade, and I curl on my side in the space between two outgrowths. I might just rest until the police come for me.

I'm awakened by Lisa. "Hey, Des, you planning on staying the night?"

I'm sweaty and groggy. "What time is it?"

"Around four-thirty. The wind started gusting to sixteen and we couldn't put the student up. Saw your car. I didn't know you were still waiting over here."

"God, I must've been knocked out."

"We're closing up in a few minutes. Nothing going on."

I thank her for waking me. Now it's too late to get home in time for Tom's call around five. I go to the pay phone, beep him, and sit down on the picnic bench to wait. In fifteen minutes, he hasn't returned the call. I'm going to have to leave when Lisa locks up. I remember how I wasn't quite welcome the first time I turned up at Tom's unexpectedly, but that was months ago, a lifetime ago. I figure I'll wait in the car if he's not there.

I get to the end of his drive and the Bronco is there. I'm relieved. I turn to pull up on the other side, but there's a Jaguar parked in my usual spot. It's a beautiful silver, seems new. I wonder if it's one of those guys who can afford to hire people to do his thinking. I'd like to meet an asshole like that who owns wild animals, just see what kind of shit he's got on the brain.

I go to the door and knock. I'm not comfortable walking in without warning. I wait. No answer. "Tom, Tom," I call. I turn the knob, but it's locked. I figure they're over by the lion cage, doing business, checking out the stock. I still feel a stab in my stomach thinking of Tom involved in this. I can rationalize homicide, apparently—but not torture of an innocent animal.

I make my way down the path, avoiding spiderwebs and swatting at the gnats around my face. The Florida hollies and vines are becoming overgrown, need trimming. I turn into the clearing. Tom and some guy in a safari hat are sitting across from each other at the picnic table, drinking beer, Tom's back is to me. He's laughing. There's a rifle lying between them. The feeling is no good. I want to turn around, but the stranger sees me immediately. I can tell by the look on his face that I've made a big mistake. I don't know what to do but keep walking.

As I get closer, I see a tarpaulin wrapped around something on the ground. My guts lurch. I know what's under the tarp. As I look closer, I see a tawny fur paw sticking out from the side. I gasp. I visualize the cub's flat, dead eyes, the bloody fur, imagine the pain as he made his last desperate movements, the bullet searing through him. I feel the pain cut into my chest.

The man continues staring at me, until Tom turns around.

"No, no, no!" I shriek, and cover my face. I can feel myself twisting, my elbows crushing my chest, my body a straining knot of pain. I'm digging into my scalp and screaming deep in my throat, like it's a dream, screaming, screaming, for the cub and for Swan, and for myself, screaming because I hate Tom and I hate myself, and it's all so clear to me too late. I drop to the ground and sit, my eyes aching and hot from lack of tears, knowing at some point I'll have to stop letting myself blubber, and then the world will begin to turn again with all the damage in place that I've enabled, that I'll have to take responsibility for. I've managed to cancel out all the work in my past, all my moral motivations. I gave in and gave up everything so easily, for so little. There's nowhere to go from here, nothing, no possibility of changing what's already done, no hope that I'll go insane or kill myself. I'll have to continue on, knowing everything, knowing what Tom is, keeping silent, hating myself.

I feel the stranger's eyes on me, his shock at my behavior, but I don't care. I don't care what this monster thinks. I visualize Big-gun's furry nose, now flattened against the ground. I dig harder with my nails and scream hoarsely, "Please, please, please, please, please . . ." It's from my soul, a primitive *please* without meaning, a scalding knife of yearning in my stomach—oh, never to have been born.

Tom steps over and takes my hand to pull me up. I slap it away. He tries again and I slap his arm, slapping, slapping with both hands—

"Stop!" He grabs my wrists hard. "Stop it!" My knees go weak, but he drags me up.

I shout in his face, "Take the rifle and shoot me! Just shoot me."

I feel the stranger go past, hear the dragging of the canvas on the ground as he hauls off his prize. A rock-hard coldness settles into my chest, and I sob, holding most of it inside. We're alone, Tom and I.

"Get ahold of yourself. Fuck. You're a big girl. Get a grip." His hands are hard on my shoulders, hurting me, and I want him to hurt me more. My nose is streaming and my jaws hurt from the wide grimace I can't control.

"Okay, that's enough. Settle down, baby. It's not such a big deal. One shot. One good shot. Better than living in captivity, some might say."

I feel my eyes nearly explode from my head from repressed anger. "You always have a rational answer, don't you?" I grit my teeth and breath hisses between them. "It was a hunt, wasn't it? Sport for some big-time fucking loser. What sport? That cub was too young—too tame—to even run."

"Oh, he ran all right. You bet he did." An instant of triumph flashes across his face for a job well done, a horror he enjoyed, before he can put the sorry look back.

I want to rasp out in hatred, but my voice dribbles down to sobs, nothing more to say, no gaps left to fill. If I still believed any of Tom's intentions or his warnings about Swan, the cub's killing has canceled out all of it, everything between us. I can feel the searing hate in my eyes, an equal glare to Tom's.

"Hey, it's a fucking animal. You need to settle down. I mean it. You turned your head at murder, and now you're gonna break down over an animal?"

I look at him. I force the words through my teeth. "It's just how sick and twisted I am." My eyes feel sharpened to points. "You know me—you played me all along, every perfect step of the way. But not anymore."

"Listen, Des, you got exactly what you wanted, and if you're smart, you'll keep on wanting it just like it is. Remember, twisted sister, it's your M-99 in her bloodstream and your fingerprints on her fucking bedpost."

"Yeah. And you were the one on the fucking plane."

He chuckles. "You know what? With any luck at all, nobody will remember that. Up and down all day—it's hard to think who you just jumped with, much less which thirty people were on the load. Nobody knew me but Swan. I was off the DZ before they found out there was a problem—and your name's on the manifest list."

I swallow. "How?"

He nods. His eyes are shining. "I manifested you instead of myself—nothing unusual. I'd say I have a good chance—and you're a goner—if there are any questions."

I begin to shake with rage, rage at myself for my stupidity.

His voice is calm, now that he's got control. "Easy, baby. Nothing's changed. You're my girl, and you're gonna stay that way.

Chill. You know me—I didn't realize he wanted a hunt. He paid big bucks for the cub—in advance. Cub's his property. Supposed to be done with it yesterday." He rubs my head roughly, holds my chin up. "What do you think— I enjoyed seeing that?"

I point to the picnic table. "Yes." My words are weak. "You were drinking a beer with him. Laughing along."

He shrugs, shakes his head. "I didn't enjoy it; I was glad all went well and the cub never suffered. It was supposed to be done while we were at Disney."

"Yeah, two murders in one day." There's no relief. I shake my head, feel poison pumping through my blood at every word.

"Hey, you work hard. Okay. But did you ever go around hungry as a kid? See what nice stuff everybody else has and wonder why you don't have anything? Wonder what's wrong with you?" He looks at me. "Yeah, yeah. It's a tough story—everybody's got one. Well, when I finally get an opportunity, I take it, and I'm not apologizing to you or some dumb animal."

I stand there silent as he walks away down the path, stunned as if hit by lightning. I've been living his interpretation of life. Lies on top of lies. I think about the dangerous things that happened, the trap set at the park and my double malfunction—all Tom's doings to scare me into murdering Swan? Pure invention. She wasn't even involved. He took me seconds away from death, egotistical enough to risk that he could save me, become my savior and take me in. He always knew what he wanted, and it wasn't me. Even his admission of murdering Swan wasn't enough to clear my eyes. Finally, the true power of his self-absorption and disregard for life takes hold of my guts as I picture the innocent cub, bloody and mangled. I'm a more deserving victim, but it isn't going to be that way. Vengeance slips into my brain, my only means of payback for Swan and all the cubs he's sold or had killed. I feel my blood come alive. It's really self-defense this time. He can't let me live unless I stay with him and keep his trust as his love slave. A sick thought, what I've already been. He's played on my needs and fears, used me so well. It won't work any longer. Not that I'm excused. I'll take my righteous punishment. We're both skygods in our selfish, destructive ways and don't deserve to live on solid ground among real people—but he'll go first.

I SIT DOWN. I NEED TO GIVE HIM A few minutes in case he's got some details with the asshole and the cub. I don't want to see anything more. I take out my drops and squirt several drops into my eyes, wipe the runoff with the back of my hand. I pick up the beer that Tom left on the table. It's half-full. I take a gulp, then finish it.

I pick myself up and head back. I realize my feelings have changed so completely, so suddenly, it's like I knew and loved a different Tom, years ago. But it's only me who's changed. I need to put on my old innocent self until I figure out what to do. I reach into my pocket. Roth's number is still there. It's a place to start. He'll be interested in the real truth about his sister's death.

I hear a car starting up, the purr of the Jaguar as the guy drives off down the road. I try not to think of the sweet feline he's probably got in a plastic bag so it doesn't leak bodily fluids into his luxurious trunk. I open the door to the trailer and I concentrate on making my face sad and forgiving.

Tom swings his head out of the kitchen. He's sizing me up.

"I'm okay now. Sorry I had such a fit. You know how I feel about animals."

"Yeah, you like them better than people."

"Better than a lot of people." I take a breath. His ego is going to help me. He doesn't even imagine that I can let him go. "Yeah. I used to say that. Sometimes animals were the only friends I cared about. But now here I am with you, and after what's happened, I guess I can't say it anymore. It was silly—immature."

He's drying his hands on a towel. "I've got a couple big porterhouse steaks. You won't have a problem eating one of those, will you?"

He takes my face in his hands, and I feel my stomach drop somewhere deep inside me. "Nope. It's all part of the cycle." I try to concentrate on his face, think of him as beautiful and mindless, what he is really. He's had it rough and he can't see beyond money. Those piercing blue eyes are fake, nothing but clouds behind them. I let myself be absorbed by his body and his ego. It's not so difficult to let him kiss me, let his lips and tongue work my mouth. The return of strong physical feeling is involuntary. My teeth go into his lip.

He pulls back, licks to see if there's blood. "You're excited by all this, aren't you, Des? I know it. I am, too. That feeling of how far you've gone, a place you never dreamed? The challenge of going there and making it back. There's something in you that thrives on it, just like me."

I nod slowly. I am feeling it, feeling a murderous high of my own. "You know all the buttons to push," I tell him.

He hands me the glass of red wine he's already poured and we toast in silence. He takes the package of steaks and leads me back outside to the grill. "Let's eat. Then I'll fuck you into daylight."

My body is in torture, with a strange combination of pain and desire, but I sit down at the picnic bench while he makes the fire. I see where the cub was dragged, the sticks and leaves pushed aside.

"You goin' back to work tomorrow?" Tom asks.

I rest my chin on my hand and make myself sound calm. "I guess I better," I tell him. "I'll have a full schedule, all the catching up. I don't know if I'll be able to skydive over the weekend."

"Good. You're getting back to normal. I have to get busy at the DZ myself."

"At least we don't have to hide out anymore—with nobody trying to kill me. Your money problems with Swan are over."

He pauses. "True. But now we have the police to think about."

"Why?" I sigh. "You said it worked perfectly."

"I know. I don't think it'll be a problem. But let's not be too bold right away at the DZ. Keep it looking casual till the pressure's off for sure."

"The people at Lake Wales know we slept in the same tent, remember?"

"Doesn't mean anything. Goes with the territory."

More clarity than I ever wanted. "Okay. I'm going to be really busy for a while. You'll be over at night, though, huh?"

"Of course. What—don't you think I love you anymore?"

I can't speak. My face screws up with the need for tears, the need to wash away the pain of self-deceiving adolescent dreams so sharply ended. But the emotion works for my deception, no crack between us. He comforts me like he still owns me.

I stay the night there. He turns out the light and moves close. I smell his skin. My body responds, the tingle of lubrication, my breath drawn hard as his hand grabs the back of my hair. He moves fast. Short kisses graze my throat in the dark, and he brushes by my nipples on the way down for a swift licking of my clitoris. I feel urgency in him—the need to get it over.

I study his strong shoulders and arms in the moonlight as he rises and penetrates me, fills the open wound that has caused all my trouble. I shudder with his expected stroke, the long pull of heaven—or in this case, hell, a hell that I've chosen again and again. I arch into him, never losing track of where I am and what he's done. I hear the groan of pleasure in my throat. He pumps until I go limp, and then he's still, a rock in his own world as he comes inside me, like clockwork. I feel myself pushed into the mattress, fire between us but no warmth. There's a stiffness in my body I can't release. My fingers are hyperextended on his arms, the tips not touching his skin. We're locked together in a vice of hate. The lovemaking is a sham on both sides. The feeling slithers into my head that he plans to kill me. Why did it take me so long to see it? I'm a threat to him as long as I live. Murder, it's necessary. The decision to kill him helps me pull myself together. I lay my face on his chest and hear his heart beating. I'm numb.

I leave very early in the morning, and relief is strong on the drive home. I unlock the door and crouch down to get smothered with wet kisses from Angel and Clue. I feel something like myself again, just a fleeting glimpse of my old self without Tom, with a firm purpose of what I have to do. I pick up the phone to call Roth, and it bleeps with messages. My heart pumps as I wait for the one that will be a homicide investigator. But no, all pet owners. The machinery of the law runs slowly, or something like that, I've heard, but the call will come, I'm sure. I don't have much to lose at this point.

I dial the number for Roth. I can't wait for his call. It's still early, but this is about murder. He picks up.

"This is Destiny. I'm sorry—"

"Destiny. I was going to call your office. I need to see you."

"Okay. As soon as possible."

"Can you meet me in Palm Beach?"

"Meet me at my office—the one at Lion Country."

He pauses. "I don't want to be seen."

"No one will be there. I don't want you to be seen, either." I give him directions for getting in the back way, and tell him to meet me at one. "I'll leave the gate unlocked." I pause. "I'm very sorry about your sister."

"Thanks. I need information from you."

"I'll be there—one, at the hospital."

I call Gerald and tell him I'll be in around noon to take care of everything for the rest of the day. He's happy to have his afternoon free again. I put down the phone and get myself in gear to see patients, maybe the last time.

I get to the park at noon and begin the fecals. It's hard to work, but one o'clock finally comes and then quarter after. He's late.

I sit there and begin to feel nervous. I'm starting to think that Tom might have heard something. Or Roth is bringing the police. I don't know what would make him late. Finally, I hear his car pull up. I unlock the door. He's sweaty and looks beat. I lead him into my office, to a chair beside my desk. I sit down and take a deep breath. Nibblefoot is looking at me with his nose twitching.

"I know Tom killed my sister. Don't waste my time—"

"You're right. I didn't ask you here to argue."

He stops. "Okay, then." He chews his lip and studies me. "I knew he had you. You were another one of his suckers—like all of us, not the kind of person in it for the money. I did some checking."

I nod, wondering how he was used by Tom. I feel the pressure in my jaw from gritting my teeth. "I didn't know about any money."

"Swan's investments, insurance—I don't know what all there is yet. Swan had built up a lot of money separate from the family's. She was a smart investor, but . . . she left it all to Tom. You could have been in on that." He shakes his head violently. A shiver lodges in my shoulders. "Our father hated that bastard. Dad's the only one who had him figured out from day one."

"She left her money to Tom? I thought they were getting a divorce?"

"She divorced him once, but she never could give him up. She just kept Tom away from our parents. They got remarried—Mexico, I think. She didn't even tell me, just her lawyer. He has the license and will. She was worried about her heart problem and didn't want Tom to be left with nothing, living in that rotting trailer. He had her convinced that he was some deprived angel—

that his heart and soul matched his looks. I didn't know how far off that was, either, until now. Well, until he tried to get me out of the way."

"When he broke your jaw?"

"Yeah. I couldn't prove anything, but I knew he did it on purpose. I've been watching him ever since, waiting until I could prove something—or get him somehow." He whacks his hand on the desk. "I waited too fucking long."

"When did he start selling lion cubs for those sickos to hunt?"

"I don't know. That's a new one on me. Whenever somebody asked him would be my guess. I wish I'd known."

"I saw it in action—almost. I fell for that 'deprived angel' shit myself, believed all his lies. It's his goddamned face."

Roth grits his teeth. His lips are curled in a sneer.

"Skygod," I said. "Opposite of angel. I know. She couldn't give him up—the ego, the sex. I know all about it." I look straight and hard at Roth. "I want to kill him."

"Yeah? I thought you might. That's two of us."

I brace myself, knowing he could take me right to the police, and I tell him the details of my attempt on Swan's life, and how Tom took over where I had failed. I watch recognition and hate pass across his face. Sorrow moves back into his eyes. "I'm responsible for letting it happen," I tell him. "I would have done it myself—he had me so convinced that she wanted to kill me. I'll do whatever you tell me to do to make up for it. I owe you and your family. I don't care what happens to me."

"It makes sense. They're saying it was her heart, the stress of the bag lock, but I knew she would have pulled her reserve. That was nothing to her. I knew Tom had done it—because he was there, because I know Tom."

"He's got all kinds of evidence that points to me—a tranquilizer, fingerprints . . ."

"Give me the details."

I describe the scenario just as Tom did when he told me. I watch the hate seethe in Roth's eyes. Tears begin to run down his face. I break into dry sobs as I describe the effects of the M-99—the poison I made available.

Roth swipes the tears from his face and takes my hand. "I feel sorry for you—he must have worked you all along."

I nod. My eyes burn. "Yeah, he scared me good, set me up—but it's no excuse."

Roth makes two fists and plants them hard on the desk. "I want to kill him. No police, no fucking chance in court. Get it done. See him dead. I want him to die like she did, no reusable organs left in his body. I want his motherfucking face smeared on the runway."

"I'll do anything. It's all I want, too."

He wipes his eyes. "I've started working on a plan. I just needed to know the details, to be sure I was right. Can I count on you to help me?"

"Tell me what to do."

Roth nods. "I have his rig in the trunk of my car. I went over there and switched it for mine. He's gone off for the afternoon, as usual."

"Probably to sell some lion cubs—or shoot some."

"Yeah. It doesn't surprise me."

"He said you got him into it."

"He used me to find buyers. I didn't realize what he was doing. It was a few years ago, when we were still friends—or so I thought. My mistake. Let's not talk about the son of a bitch. I get livid."

"You have the same color rig?"

"We were on a team together, me, Tom, Swan, and another guy. I'm going to pack him a double malfunction that looks accidental. I'll need you to make sure he uses the sabotaged rig. I'll have to break off his seal from the last repack he did. Can you get his sealer so I can put another one back on? I want to make it look like he packed for his own death trip."

"No problem. He keeps his packing tools in his truck."

"It might seem coincidental so soon after Swan's death, but nobody will be able to prove anything."

"I'll confess if they do," I tell him. I pick up a pellet and hold it where Nibblefoot can grab it. She stows it in a corner of the cage. "I know how to fix him so they'll never suspect. It'll put you in the clear."

"You're not a rigger."

"You can help me. I want to do this. It'll give me satisfaction, sort of a chance for the animal kingdom to get back at him. They deserve to."

"How?"

I point to Nibble's cage. "Let's just take out a few lines and let Nibblefoot work on them overnight."

"The rat?"

"Yeah. Nibblefoot. She'll chew them into fuzz, no problem." I laugh. I'm near hysterics. "It's my satisfaction really. Animals are pure."

"I see. So when Tom pulls his reserve, the lines will snap—if they're not already completely chewed."

"It'll look like something got in there. A freak accident, no chance of survival."

"You're right—nobody would think of it. But it's packed too damn tight. Nothing could get in there, except ants."

"People always say that—'Nothing could have gotten in there'—after it has. So maybe they'll think it's ants. A small mouse maybe. If Forensics does an analysis, they'll find rodent saliva. Doubt if they'd question further."

"If they do, they'll go straight to you—then to me."

I shrug. "Let them have me. I'll tell them Tom taught me how to pack a reserve."

"They won't believe you."

"I'll be as convincing as I can. That's your risk."

"It's my risk either way. I'll take it."

Roth brings in the rig, sets it on my desk, and takes out the reserve. We stuff as many lines through the cage bars as will fit. Nibble just looks at us from the corner of the cage, but I know as soon as we're gone she'll hobble over and have a ball, make herself a rat's nest.

"I'll reroute the bridle on the main to give old Tom a nice container lock."

"Yeah. I figured."

His face gets red, something between anger and pain. I know he's reliving what Tom did to Swan. "You knew about that?"

"Not until afterward, but I'm just as guilty. Tom told me all sorts of lies, and I sucked them right up. He convinced me she was trying to kill me."

"That's ridiculous."

"I had her mixed up with somebody else—big mistake—and Tom played right along with it." I cross my arms and hold my shoulders. The full realization of my weakness washes over me. "He knew exactly how to get into my soul." I shudder. "We have to do this fast, before he sees through me."

"Tomorrow. Can I come here in the morning to do the packing? I don't want to be dragging an open canopy around."

"No problem—if you go early."

"Then I can switch the rigs when he goes for lunch. Here's a key. Number three at that little motel right down the road from your office—Lee told me where you were, so I've been checking things out. Drop off his seal there tonight so I can do the repack in the morning."

"I can walk the dogs down there. What if he jumps your rig before you get his put back?"

Roth looks at the container. "He won't notice. We have exactly the same size, same canopy, both clean. I made the switch while a load was up. Nobody saw me go in or out."

"You all used to be a pretty close group, huh?"

"Yeah, but even then Tom had a chip on his shoulder." He runs his hands over his dark unshaved chin, chews at his thumbnail.

"Who was the other person?"

"Damn nice guy—died. He was in love with Swan—everybody is—was—but she was always stuck on Tom."

I see his eyes get glassy, so I let the subject drop, but I'm wondering if the guy had the computer malfunction that Tom mentioned. I'm suspicious of everything, too late.

I put my hand on his arm. He's shaking, not the cocky Roth I met at the DZ weeks ago, a lifetime ago. "You need to get done and out of here before seven in the morning, when the other vet comes in. Put the keys under the little cage outside when you leave. I'll get them in the afternoon. I'm going to ask Tom to jump with me on the sunset load. I'll accidentally pull the handle on his other rig so he'll have to use this one."

"That'll work."

"I want to see the look on his face when he realizes that Destiny has taken revenge."

"Yeah? It has a nice ring to it, but watch out. He's an expert in the air. He'll get ahold of you and take you down with him."

"I'll take the risk." I shrug.

I walk Roth out the door, look around to make sure nobody's there. "Clouding up," I say. "I'd better get going. Tom's coming over for dinner tonight—with the clouds, he could be early."

Roth tilts his head. "No, it's beautiful over that way. Look at all the holes."

As I follow his gaze, shivers run down my back. Those were the words Tom had used when I mentioned all the clouds one day. I thought it was his original thought, significant of his love of life and positive outlook. Another fake, more bait. A harsh rasp of a laugh comes up from my throat. "I can't wait till it's done."

"I don't want to see Tom until he's chowder."

I GET HOME AND THERE'S A MES-
sage from a police investigator. He wants me to call him back. I hope he's not too eager.

I've rented a movie for the night, so I don't have to do much talking. I feel stiff when Tom comes in and I try to kiss him. I go into the kitchen to cook while he relaxes and has a beer. Normally, I would ask about his day, but now I know most of what he says is a lie. I can't take it. I start a salad, cut up onions, feel the burn in my dry eyes. He stays in the living room, watching some game. Probably glad not to talk about Swan.

I begin to buck up, like a suicidal person when the final decision is made and everything's in order. No more wondering and hopeless wishing, no more wrestling, all decided, all done—Destiny done. I always knew I'd find a meaning for that.

I fix lasagna, since it's his favorite—his would-be request were he to know it's his last meal. I carry that thought with me into dinner, and I smile as he takes his first big bite, twirling the stringy mozzarella around his fork, getting some sauce on the side of his mouth. His eyes have a sparkle in them. I wonder what his plan is for me. No hurry maybe—as long as I play my part. "Good. Delicious," he says.

I chew and swallow, smile big. "Will you jump with me tomorrow afternoon? I need some pointers."

"Sure, if I'm not too busy."

"I want to work a few hours catch-up, but I can make the sunset load. What about that?"

"Yeah. It'll be crowded. We've got a big group from Switzerland. Weather's supposed to be great."

"I need you to help me practice a few things in freefall."

"I'll manifest you earlier. Otherwise, they'll have all the slots."

"You'll be there?"

"Yeah. Sure. I have some business after lunch, but I'll go back to the DZ around four."

I smile and enjoy every bite of my dinner. He has no idea of the murder I have in me. When we finish, I let Clue and Angel lick the plates. I put the dishes into the sink. I'll probably never have to do them. I put *Titanic* into the VCR and curl up next to Tom in his clean-smelling T-shirt. I can't help thinking that this is what normal life would have been like. So what? It's never much anyway, all lies and foolish dreams to make you keep on living. Revenge is a much more fulfilling feeling than I expected.

I fall asleep during the movie and wake up for the credits. The iceberg's come and gone, Tom's asleep, snoring lightly, and all those lives have been lost at sea. I take a bag and go out to his truck to get his seal. By the time he would look for it, he'll be gone. I set it behind the bushes and go in to get the dogs for a walk. It's half a mile to the hotel. Their lucky night.

We walk fast and I'm sweating when we get to the room. I open the door and let the dogs in with me. The air's on, but there's no sign of Roth or the rig. I set the bag on the bed and leave the key. It's creepy.

When I get home, Tom is still asleep in front of the TV and everything is normal. I shake him and he gets up from the couch and walks to the bedroom, still groggy. He pulls off his clothes and we curl next to each other for the last time. I feel the heat coming off of me, but it's a new kind of desire.

When I get to the hospital, the keys are under the cage and the rig is gone. Nibblefoot seems normal. There's no thread or fuzz. I can only assume that everything went right. No messages from Roth.

I find myself calm and able to do some work, in a level mood. I get all the stool samples done, plenty of worming, and a drive-around check. I feel good about myself. It could be my last day of work, one way or another. I want to leave a fine record.

I get to the DZ a little after four, but Tom's not there, and we're not manifested. I go ahead and manifest. Dolly's working and she assumes Tom is in the hangar. I see how easy it is. I go back to his office. Both rigs are hanging on pegs by the doorway. I stroke the smooth blue-and-white container, wondering what kind of snarl is inside. I realize it will be easier to pull his reserve handle on the other rig now and make up a story when he gets there—clumsiness, whatever. I give it a yank, out and down, and the pilot chute pops up and whacks me in the face. Fuck. It hurts where the hard spring hit above the eye. Stupid. I rub my forehead. Nothing broken to stop me from jumping. I'll have a swollen red mark to add convincing foolishness to my action.

I sit in the chair in front of Tom's video equipment to wait. I've never watched one of his videos or seen him land with the camera on his head—he just has to have everything, try it all. I bet Swan paid for it.

The door creaks open and I jolt.

Tom comes around the corner. "Hey, dollface, sorry I'm late. Did you manifest?" He bends to give me a kiss. "What happened? You already do a jump?"

"No. I hate to tell you."

"You okay? Looks like you caught a heel in freefall. What?"

I point to the right, the pilot chute on the floor. It's partially hidden behind a cabinet, hanging out of his rig with a clump of lines.

"Shit. How'd you do that?"

"Accident. Moronic. I tripped over my own two feet and grabbed for something, caught your handle."

He touches the spot above my eye. "Good aim with that pilot chute."

"Now you have to put it back together. I'm sorry."

"No big deal. I have the other rig. This one's almost due for a repack anyway. I'll do it all tomorrow."

"Hope you have time."

"Plenty of time. I feel like my life is just beginning."

I smile the best I can. I know that he means now that Swan is dead and he can plan on a ton of money coming in. It's sickening. I look at him and want the pleasure of seeing inevitable death grow solid in those thunderous eyes. As he moves close, I stand and tilt my face up for his kiss. My mouth cooperates—my body is a traitor, as always, with him.

The announcement comes over the speaker for load nineteen, our twenty minute call. "I better get set up. I haven't set aside my rental."

"Not a problem. No other renters here today." He turns me by the shoulders and swats my ass. "Git a move on, lady. Meet me under the tree to dirt dive."

I go to the rack, but my usual rig is missing. Must be in for repairs or a repack. Lee gives me the 220 Navigator, huge for me, but I've jumped in it several times. He tells me not to worry—there's no wind to blow me backward. That's the last thing to worry about. I pick out a helmet and goggles. Hope Tom's getting ready. I get my jumpsuit from the locker and try to concentrate on getting it on right. My fingers are shaking, so it's hard to thread the chest strap through the buckle. I take a deep breath and try to calm down, thinking of my first time, the exhilaration when the chute opened. I've come a long way in getting the control to move in all directions—to fly—a learning process about myself and my fears.

Now it will end. There's nothing left to learn about myself anyway. I'm a monster.

I walk at a determined pace out to the tree. Tom is waiting. "Don't look so serious. Relax."

"So much has happened, you know? Seems like a long time since I've jumped the Porter. Hope I haven't forgotten how to exit."

"We can go out together. You'll be stable." He walks me through a series of moves and gives me tips on my body position. He'll maintain a heading and I'll work my way around him, something we've done before, but good practice for keeping relative and moving forward, he tells me.

"When we break, could you watch my tracking?" I ask him. "I can't tell if I'm getting anywhere, and I always feel like I'm turning to one side."

"Yeah. Break at four. I'll watch until you pull."

I'm thinking of him watching me, looking for flaws in my body position so he can tell me how to correct the next time. He's devoted to skydiving. Innocent in trying to help me. No inkling of my feelings. How is it possible?

His eyes are as clear as the sky and the breeze tosses his hair with glints of gold. Everything is perfect. All that glitters . . . I tell myself. We're alone on the picnic bench under the tree. The Swiss team are still on creepers in the hangar, perfecting their moves.

Tom points to the plane as it pulls up to the gas pump. "I didn't know he had to fuel. We've got a few minutes." He puts an arm over the top of my rig and tickles my neck with his finger. "The reason I was late—I stopped at the attorney's office."

"You got a lawyer? What happened?"

"No, no. Everything's fine. In fact, it's grand—much more than grand, close to a million."

"A million?"

"Dollars, sweetheart. Swan left me a large portion of her investments. Your fucking boyfriend is a wealthy man."

My mouth falls open. I can't believe he'd tell me about the money. Either he trusts me or he's already got a plan to kill me and feels like bragging in the meantime. "I guess you can stop hunting cubs now."

"Yeah. Can we forget about that? It's over. You haven't changed since the day we met."

"I wish I could agree." I put my hand up for a high five and slap his palm hard. "Done. Forgotten."

"So what's the first thing you're gonna buy? A brand-new rig?"

"Me?"

"Yeah, you. What'd you think? I'm ready to dump you? You're not leaving, are you? It wouldn't be any fun spending the money without you."

"Really?"

"We're bound together as tight as two people can get—your dream come true and all the money you could want. You never have to smear another slide with shit."

I'm feeling light-headed. I can't figure out why he's slathering on the honey when it's not necessary. There's something in me that still wants to believe him. He pulls me in for a long kiss. A cloud floats into my brain. I don't have to kill Tom. Maybe he does love me and wants to share his life and fortune. I've never had an offer like this.

The Porter starts up again and moves forward across the runway. Now's the time if I'm going to cancel the jump. I look at Tom, his hair dappled by sun through the leaves, eyes bluer than anything in nature, bluer than truth. He's too much for me and for the world. I can't make the U-turn this time.

The plane rolls to the pickup area, and I begin to walk, zombielike.

"Buck up, Bucko." Tom gives me a thumbs-up and a brilliant grin. I smile back the best I can. We wait at the plane and climb in last to get out first, since the Swiss have a six-way, which will fall slower. They're five men and a woman. I envy her, her apparent confidence. If things were different—if I were different—I'd be there someday, flying my slot, living in those moments, nothing else in the world, pulling together for each point.

Tom is sitting behind me to spot, so I don't have to look at him. My hands are resting lightly on his legs, which are bent under each of my arms. The sweat runs down my back inside my jumpsuit. It's a long ride to 12,500.

The pilot calls, "Door," and Tom reaches past me and slides it back, leans out to get a clear view past the step. My throat is tight, guts clenched.

"Cut." Tom turns toward me, his back to the outside, as we planned. My mind clears and I face him, grab his chest strap, and get ready to push. He rocks to the count: "Ready, set, go." I push us out and we flatten on the air together, beautiful, perfect. I let go of his chest strap and he takes my wrists. I feel myself smiling. He moves forward for a kiss and I'm flooded with exhilaration despite myself.

He lets go and I fly to the right mechanically, around him, touching his thigh grip, his calves, his thigh on the other side, back to the beginning, the best I've ever done. I start over. This is the longest minute of my life. I make it around again, and he grabs my wrists and holds me as we drop through a cloud. The cool white mist surrounds us. I glance at my altimeter and see six thousand feet, ten seconds till we break apart and I track away as fast as I can. My feelings have changed. I'm not enjoying the anticipation of his death after all. I don't want to see him when the cold truth invades the sapphire of his eyes and terror contorts the last beautiful moments of his face.

My altimeter hits four thousand and Tom lets go. I shoot forward and grab his chest strap with both hands. I can't make myself turn from him to get away. He motions for me to break. I can't move. He's searching my face, motioning again, his eyes neon blue ice. The needle is on the three thousand mark and he grabs my wrists. I shake my head, mouth the word *no*, and tilt my head toward his pilot chute. I pull myself to his body.

Finally, he understands that he's rigged to die, knows I've set him up, and now I can't let him go alone. But there's no fear in his face, only determination. He hugs me close, crawling half under me, and I feel him ramming his arms between me and my rig. I don't know if he can hold on when the chute jolts open, or if my canopy is big enough to carry us both, but I have to try. I whip out the pilot chute, long seconds of nothing. I watch for a lifetime as the canopy jerks out and undulates above me, one, two, three . . . springs open. Tom's weight is tremendous on my body, my backbone crushed in his locked arms. His face is smothered in my chest, legs wrapped around the backs of my knees. His words come out muffled. "Release the brakes."

I peel the toggles off the Velcro and give each a pull. We're flying fast, already at five hundred feet. I can barely breathe, but I'm thinking of how to land. There's nothing else. The spot is good and we're right above the student field. Tom is silent. He can't see ahead and he's using all his strength to hang on. My lungs are on the verge of collapse.

As I flare, he raises his legs and we hit the ground in a roll, me tumbling over him, and him over me, again and again, until we flop down flat, me on top with a mass of twisted risers, lines, canopy.

Tom pulls his arms from under my rig. I slowly stand. Nothing hurts. I feel absolutely nothing. He looks up at me from the ground, a vision of amazement, with the most beautiful face I've ever seen. I stoop and begin gathering the canopy, then stop and get a breath. Tom is still sitting on the grass, staring at me with something like wonder. The sun is an apricot ball on the horizon beyond, gilding the fields of waving sugar and catching the tips of his hair in sparks. It's over. I'm solidly relieved I didn't kill him, and glad I haven't followed Grandma to the other side, but I have no feeling for him. The primitive response from deep in my cells is the pure pleasure of being alive. A million or no million—it makes no difference. I've done the right thing. From this point on, no lies. I tuck the pilot chute and bag into the center of the canopy and wad it together in my arms, avoiding Tom's eyes as he tries to stand. He's having a problem with one ankle. I pull off my helmet and goggles, turn, and walk away from him, heading toward the hangar.

There's a local police car parked near the manifest building. The small amount of air I have left goes out of my body. Could it be one of the cops who skydives, stopped by on duty? I doubt it. Never saw the car here before. I keep walking, glance to see that Tom is limping at a distance behind me. Tomcat. He calls my name. I don't stop. His voice gets farther and farther away, lower. "Des, Destiny? Wait. We need to talk."

I can tell by his tone that he hasn't given up. He still expects to keep me silent with his irresistible charm. I look back. "Destiny waits for no one." I shake my head. "I'm not your Destiny any-more." I let out a sharp laugh at my pun—and at myself for all my stupidity. I was never his, never would be.

He stops calling. There's the flap of nylon as the others land behind and beside me in the field—the Swiss team, touching down lightly, peacefully, rich in adrenaline, having outsmarted death once again. I keep walking. A uniformed policeman steps out from the side of the building. Nobody I know. Maybe Roth called them. No sense thinking about it.

I look up at the sky and inhale my last dreamy breath of it for a long time, maybe forever. Rose-tinged cumulus clouds form a mountain range from north to south across the horizon, and white billows mound toward the east. But the holes are there—plenty of holes—waiting for someone else to jump through them.